AN ALCOTT CHRISTMAS COLLECTION

A Christmas Dream, A Country Christmas, Excerpts from Little Women, & More

LOUISA MAY ALCOTT

This work is a product of its time and place and may include values, images, events, and language that are offensive to modern sensibilities. Reader discretion is advised.

"A Christmas Dream, And How It Came True" appeared in *The Louisa May Alcott Reader* in 1908 and is in the public domain

"A Merry Christmas" is an excerpt from *Little Women*, which was originally published in 1868-69, and is in the public domain.

"Tessa's Surprises" and "Tilly's Christmas" were originally published in *Aunt Jo's Scrap-Bag, Volume I* in 1882 and is in the public domain.

"A Country Christmas" and "What the Bells Saw and Said" were originally published in *Proverb Stories* in 1882 and is in the public domain.

"A Christmas Turkey, and How It Came" appeared in *Harper's Young People*, on December 22, 1885, and is in the public domain.

No copyright claim is made with respect to public domain works.

This work reflects minor editorial revisions to the original texts.

Cover design created using Canva.com and reproduced pursuant to its free media license agreement.

CONTENTS

A Christmas Dream, And How It Came True	1
A Merry Christmas	17
Tessa's Surprises	29
Tilly's Christmas	41
A Country Christmas	47
What the Bells Saw and Said	79
A Christmas Turkey, and How It Came	91

A CHRISTMAS DREAM, AND HOW IT CAME TRUE

"I'm so tired of Christmas I wish there never would be another one!" exclaimed a discontented-looking little girl, as she sat idly watching her mother arrange a pile of gifts two days before they were to be given.

"Why, Effie, what a dreadful thing to say! You are as bad as old Scrooge; and I'm afraid something will happen to you, as it did to him, if you don't care for dear Christmas," answered mamma, almost dropping the silver horn she was filling with delicious candies.

"Who was Scrooge? What happened to him?" asked Effie, with a glimmer of interest in her listless face, as she picked out the sourest lemon-drop she could find; for nothing sweet suited her just then.

"He was one of Dickens's best people, and you can read the charming story some day. He hated Christmas until a strange dream showed him how dear and beautiful it was, and made a better man of him."

"I shall read it; for I like dreams, and have a great many curious ones myself. But they don't keep me from being tired of Christmas," said Effie, poking discontentedly among the sweeties for something worth eating.

"Why are you tired of what should be the happiest time of all the year?" asked mamma, anxiously.

"Perhaps I shouldn't be if I had something new. But it is always the same, and there isn't any more surprise about it. I always find heaps of goodies in my stocking. Don't like some of them, and soon get tired of those I do like. We always have a great dinner, and I eat too much, and feel ill next day. Then there is a Christmas tree somewhere, with a doll on top, or a stupid old Santa Claus, and children dancing and screaming over bonbons and toys that break, and shiny things that are of no use. Really, mamma, I've had so many Christmases all alike that I don't think I *can* bear another one." And Effie laid herself flat on the sofa, as if the mere idea was too much for her.

Her mother laughed at her despair, but was sorry to see her little girl so discontented, when she had everything to make her happy, and had known but ten Christmas days.

"Suppose we don't give you *any* presents at all,--how would that suit you?" asked mamma, anxious to please her spoiled child.

"I should like one large and splendid one, and one dear little one, to remember some very nice person by," said Effie, who was a fanciful little body, full of odd whims and notions, which her friends loved to gratify, regardless of time, trouble, or money; for she was the last of three little girls, and very dear to all the family.

"Well, my darling, I will see what I can do to please you, and not say a word until all is ready. If I could only get a new idea to start with!" And mamma went on tying up her pretty bundles with a thoughtful face, while Effie strolled to the window to watch the rain that kept her in-doors and made her dismal.

"Seems to me poor children have better times than rich ones. I can't go out, and there is a girl about my age splashing along, without any maid to fuss about rubbers and cloaks and umbrellas and colds. I wish I was a beggar-girl."

"Would you like to be hungry, cold, and ragged, to beg all day, and sleep on an ash-heap at night?" asked mamma, wondering what would come next.

"Cinderella did, and had a nice time in the end. This girl out here has a basket of scraps on her arm, and a big old shawl all round her, and doesn't seem to care a bit, though the water runs out of the toes of her boots. She goes paddling along, laughing at the rain, and eating a cold potato as if it tasted nicer than the chicken and ice-cream I had for dinner. Yes, I do think poor children are happier than rich ones."

"So do I, sometimes. At the Orphan Asylum today I saw two dozen merry little souls who have no parents, no home, and no hope of Christmas beyond a stick of candy or a cake. I wish you had been there to see how happy they were, playing with the old toys some richer children had sent them."

"You may give them all mine; I'm so tired of them I never want to see them again," said Effie, turning from the window to the pretty baby-house full of everything a child's heart could desire.

"I will, and let you begin again with something you will not tire of, if I can only find it." And mamma knit her brows trying to discover some grand surprise for this child who didn't care for Christmas.

Nothing more was said then; and wandering off to the library, Effie found "A Christmas Carol," and curling herself up in the sofa corner, read it all before tea. Some of it she did not understand; but she laughed and cried over many parts of the charming story, and felt better without knowing why.

All the evening she thought of poor Tiny Tim, Mrs. Cratchit with the pudding, and the stout old gentleman who danced so gayly that "his legs twinkled in the air." Presently bedtime arrived.

"Come, now, and toast your feet," said Effie's nurse, "while I do your pretty hair and tell stories."

"I'll have a fairy tale to-night, a very interesting one," commanded Effie, as she put on her blue silk wrapper and little fur-lined slippers to sit before the fire and have her long curls brushed.

So Nursey told her best tales; and when at last the child lay down under her lace curtains, her head was full of a curious jumble of Christmas elves, poor children, snow-storms, sugarplums, and surprises. So it is no wonder that she dreamed all night; and this was the dream, which she never quite forgot.

She found herself sitting on a stone, in the middle of a great field, all alone. The snow was falling fast, a bitter wind whistled by, and night was coming on. She felt hungry, cold, and tired, and did not know where to go nor what to do.

"I wanted to be a beggar-girl, and now I am one; but I don't like it, and wish somebody would come and take care of me. I don't know who I am, and I think I must be lost," thought Effie, with the curious interest one takes in one's self in dreams.

But the more she thought about it, the more bewildered she felt. Faster fell the snow, colder blew the wind, darker grew the night; and poor Effie made up her mind that she was quite forgotten and left to freeze alone. The tears were chilled on her cheeks, her feet felt like icicles, and her heart died within her, so hungry, frightened, and forlorn was she. Laying her head on her knees, she gave herself up for lost, and sat there with the great flakes fast turning her to a little white mound, when suddenly the sound of music reached her, and starting up, she looked and listened with all her eyes and ears.

Far away a dim light shone, and a voice was heard singing. She tried to run toward the welcome glimmer, but could not stir, and stood like a small statue of expectation while the light drew nearer, and the sweet words of the song grew clearer.

From our happy home
Through the world we roam
One week in all the year,
Making winter spring

*With the joy we bring,
For Christmas-tide is here.*

*Now the eastern star
Shines from afar
To light the poorest home;
Hearts warmer grow,
Gifts freely flow,
For Christmas-tide has come.*

*Now gay trees rise
Before young eyes,
Abloom with tempting cheer;
Blithe voices sing,
And blithe bells ring,
For Christmas-tide is here.*

*Oh, happy chime,
Oh, blessed time,
That draws us all so near!
"Welcome, dear day,"
All creatures say,
For Christmas-tide is here.*

A child's voice sang, a child's hand carried the little candle; and in the circle of soft light it shed, Effie saw a pretty child coming to her through the night and snow. A rosy, smiling creature, wrapped in white fur, with a wreath of green and scarlet holly on its shining hair, the magic candle in one hand, and the other outstretched as if to shower gifts and warmly press all other hands.

Effie forgot to speak as this bright vision came nearer, leaving no trace of footsteps in the snow, only lighting the way with its little candle, and filling the air with the music of its song.

"Dear child, you are lost, and I have come to find you," said the stranger, taking Effie's cold hands in his, with a smile like sunshine, while every holly berry glowed like a little fire.

"Do you know me?" asked Effie, feeling no fear, but a great gladness, at his coming.

"I know all children, and go to find them; for this is my holiday, and I gather them from all parts of the world to be merry with me once a year."

"Are you an angel?" asked Effie, looking for the wings.

"No; I am a Christmas spirit, and live with my mates in a pleasant place, getting ready for our holiday, when we are let out to roam about the world, helping make this a happy time for all who will let us in. Will you come and see how we work?"

"I will go anywhere with you. Don't leave me again," cried Effie, gladly.

"First I will make you comfortable. That is what we love to do. You are cold, and you shall be warm, hungry, and I will feed you; sorrowful, and I will make you gay."

With a wave of his candle all three miracles were wrought,--for the snow- flakes turned to a white fur cloak and hood on Effie's head and shoulders, a bowl of hot soup came sailing to her lips, and vanished when she had eagerly drunk the last drop; and suddenly the dismal field changed to a new world so full of wonders that all her troubles were forgotten in a minute.

Bells were ringing so merrily that it was hard to keep from dancing. Green garlands hung on the walls, and every tree was a Christmas tree full of toys, and blazing with candles that never went out.

In one place many little spirits sewed like mad on warm clothes, turning off work faster than any sewing-machine ever invented, and great piles were made ready to be sent to poor people. Other busy creatures packed money into purses, and wrote checks which they sent flying away on the wind,--a lovely kind of snow-storm to fall into a world below full of poverty.

Older and graver spirits were looking over piles of little books, in which the records of the past year were kept, telling how different people had spent it, and what sort of gifts they deserved. Some got peace, some disappointment, some remorse and sorrow, some great joy and hope. The rich had generous thoughts sent them; the poor, gratitude and contentment. Children had more love and duty to parents; and parents renewed patience, wisdom, and satisfaction for and in their children. No one was forgotten.

"Please tell me what splendid place this is?" asked Effie, as soon as she could collect her wits after the first look at all these astonishing things.

"This is the Christmas world; and here we work all the year round, never tired of getting ready for the happy day. See, these are the saints just setting off; for some have far to go, and the children must not be disappointed."

As he spoke the spirit pointed to four gates, out of which four great sleighs were just driving, laden with toys, while a jolly old Santa Claus sat in the middle of each, drawing on his mittens and tucking up his wraps for a long cold drive.

"Why, I thought there was only one Santa Claus, and even he was a humbug," cried Effie, astonished at the sight.

"Never give up your faith in the sweet old stones, even after you come to see that they are only the pleasant shadow of a lovely truth."

Just then the sleighs went off with a great jingling of bells and pattering of reindeer hoofs, while all the spirits gave a cheer that was heard in the lower world, where people said, "Hear the stars sing."

"I never will say there isn't any Santa Claus again. Now, show me more."

"You will like to see this place, I think, and may learn something here perhaps."

The spirit smiled as he led the way to a little door, through which Effie peeped into a world of dolls. Baby-houses were in full blast, with dolls of all sorts going on like live people. Waxen ladies sat in their parlors elegantly dressed; black dolls cooked in the kitchens; nurses walked out with the bits of dollies; and the streets were full of tin soldiers marching, wooden horses prancing, express wagons rumbling, and little men hurrying to and fro. Shops were there, and tiny people buying legs of mutton, pounds of tea, mites of clothes, and everything dolls use or wear or want.

But presently she saw that in some ways the dolls improved upon the manners and customs of human beings, and she watched eagerly to learn why they did these things. A fine Paris doll driving in her carriage took up a black worsted Dinah who was hobbling along with a basket of clean clothes, and carried her to her journey's end, as if it were the proper thing to do. Another interesting china lady took off her comfortable red cloak and put it round a poor wooden creature done up in a paper shift, and so badly painted that its face would have sent some babies into fits.

"Seems to me I once knew a rich girl who didn't give her things to poor girls. I wish I could remember who she was, and tell her to be as kind as that china doll," said Effie, much touched at the sweet way the pretty creature wrapped up the poor fright, and then ran off in her little gray gown to buy a shiny fowl stuck on a wooden platter for her invalid mother's dinner.

"We recall these things to people's minds by dreams. I think the girl you speak of won't forget this one." And the spirit smiled, as if he enjoyed some joke which she did not see.

A little bell rang as she looked, and away scampered the children into the red-and-green school-house with the roof that lifted up, so one could see how nicely they sat at their desks with mites of books, or drew on the inch-square blackboards with crumbs of chalk.

"They know their lessons very well, and are as still as mice. We make a great racket at our school, and get bad marks every day. I shall tell the girls they had better mind what they do, or their dolls will be better scholars than they are," said Effie, much impressed, as she peeped in and saw no rod in the hand of the little mistress, who looked up and shook her head at the intruder, as if begging her to go away before the order of the school was disturbed.

Effie retired at once, but could not resist one look in at the window of a fine mansion, where the family were at dinner, the children behaved so well at table, and never grumbled a bit when their mamma said they could not have any more fruit.

"Now, show me something else," she said, as they came again to the low door that led out of Doll-land.

"You have seen how we prepare for Christmas; let me show you where we love best to send our good and happy gifts," answered the spirit, giving her his hand again.

"I know. I've seen ever so many," began Effie, thinking of her own Christmases.

"No, you have never seen what I will show you. Come away, and remember what you see to-night."

Like a flash that bright world vanished, and Effie found herself in a part of the city she had never seen before. It was far away from the gayer places, where every store was brilliant with lights and full of pretty things, and every house wore a festival air, while people hurried to and fro with merry greetings. It was down among the dingy streets where the poor lived, and where there was no making ready for Christmas.

Hungry women looked in at the shabby shops, longing to buy meat and bread, but empty pockets forbade. Tipsy men drank up their wages in the bar- rooms; and in many cold dark chambers little children huddled under the thin blankets, trying to forget their misery in sleep.

No nice dinners filled the air with savory smells, no gay trees dropped toys and bonbons into eager hands, no little stockings hung in rows beside the chimney-piece ready to be filled, no happy sounds of music, gay voices, and dancing feet were heard; and there were no signs of Christmas anywhere.

"Don't they have any in this place?" asked Effie, shivering, as she held fast the spirit's hand, following where he led her.

"We come to bring it. Let me show you our best workers." And the spirit pointed to some sweet-faced men and women who came stealing into the poor houses, working such beautiful miracles that Effie could only stand and watch.

Some slipped money into the empty pockets, and sent the happy mothers to buy all the comforts they needed; others led the drunken men out of temptation, and took them home to find safer pleasures there. Fires were kindled on cold hearths, tables spread as if by magic, and warm clothes wrapped round shivering limbs. Flowers suddenly bloomed in the chambers of the sick; old people found themselves remembered; sad hearts were consoled by a tender word, and wicked ones softened by the story of Him who forgave all sin.

But the sweetest work was for the children; and Effie held her breath to watch these human fairies hang up and fill the little stockings without which a child's Christmas is not perfect, putting in things that once she would have thought very humble presents, but which now seemed beautiful and precious because these poor babies had nothing.

"That is so beautiful! I wish I could make merry Christmases as these good people do, and be loved and thanked as they are," said Effie, softly, as she watched the busy men and women do their work and steal away without thinking of any reward but their own satisfaction.

"You can if you will. I have shown you the way. Try it, and see how happy your own holiday will be hereafter."

As he spoke, the spirit seemed to put his arms about her, and vanished with a kiss.

"Oh, stay and show me more!" cried Effie, trying to hold him fast.

"Darling, wake up, and tell me why you are smiling in your sleep," said a voice in her ear; and opening her eyes, there was mamma bending over her, and morning sunshine streaming into the room.

"Are they all gone? Did you hear the bells? Wasn't it splendid?" she asked, rubbing her eyes, and looking about her for the pretty child who was so real and sweet.

"You have been dreaming at a great rate,--talking in your sleep, laughing, and clapping your hands as if you were cheering some one. Tell me what was so splendid," said mamma, smoothing the tumbled hair and lifting up the sleepy head.

Then, while she was being dressed, Effie told her dream, and Nursey thought it very wonderful; but mamma smiled to see how curiously things the child had thought, read, heard, and seen through the day were mixed up in her sleep.

"The spirit said I could work lovely miracles if I tried; but I don't know how to begin, for I have no magic candle to make feasts appear, and light up groves of Christmas trees, as he did," said Effie, sorrowfully.

"Yes, you have. We will do it! we will do it!" And clapping her hands, mamma suddenly began to dance all over the room as if she had lost her wits.

"How? how? You must tell me, mamma," cried Effie, dancing after her, and ready to believe anything possible when she remembered the adventures of the past night.

"I've got it! I've got it!--the new idea. A splendid one, if I can only carry it out!" And mamma waltzed the little girl round till her curls flew wildly in the air, while Nursey laughed as if she would die.

"Tell me! tell me!" shrieked Effie. "No, no; it is a surprise,--a grand surprise for Christmas day!" sung mamma, evidently charmed with her happy thought. "Now, come to breakfast; for we must work like bees if we want to play spirits tomorrow. You and Nursey will go out shopping, and get heaps of things, while I arrange matters behind the scenes."

They were running downstairs as mamma spoke, and Effie called out breathlessly,--

"It won't be a surprise; for I know you are going to ask some poor children here, and have a tree or something. It won't be like my dream; for they had ever so many trees, and more children than we can find anywhere."

"There will be no tree, no party, no dinner, in this house at all, and no presents for you. Won't that be a surprise?" And mamma laughed at Effie's bewildered face.

"Do it. I shall like it, I think; and I won't ask any questions, so it will all burst upon me when the time comes," she said; and she ate her breakfast thoughtfully, for this really would be a new sort of Christmas.

All that morning Effie trotted after Nursey in and out of shops, buying dozens of barking dogs, woolly lambs, and squeaking birds; tiny tea-sets, gay picture-books, mittens and hoods, dolls and candy. Parcel after parcel was sent home; but when Effie returned she saw no trace of them, though she peeped everywhere. Nursey chuckled, but wouldn't give a hint, and went out again in the afternoon with a long list of more things to buy; while Effie wandered forlornly about the house, missing the usual merry stir that went before the Christmas dinner and the evening fun.

As for mamma, she was quite invisible all day, and came in at night so tired that she could only lie on the sofa to rest, smiling as if some very pleasant thought made her happy in spite of weariness.

"Is the surprise going on all right?" asked Effie, anxiously; for it seemed an immense time to wait till another evening came.

"Beautifully! better than I expected; for several of my good friends are helping, or I couldn't have done it as I wish. I know you will like it, dear, and long remember this new way of making Christmas merry."

Mamma gave her a very tender kiss, and Effie went to bed.

The next day was a very strange one; for when she woke there was no stocking to examine, no pile of gifts under her napkin, no one said "Merry Christmas!" to her, and the dinner was just as usual to her. Mamma vanished again, and Nursey kept wiping her eyes and saying: "The dear things! It's the prettiest idea I ever heard of. No one but your blessed ma could have done it."

"Do stop, Nursey, or I shall go crazy because I don't know the secret!" cried Effie, more than once; and she kept her eye on the clock, for at seven in the evening the surprise was to come off.

The longed-for hour arrived at last, and the child was too excited to ask questions when Nurse put on her cloak and hood, led her to the carriage, and they drove away, leaving their house the one dark and silent one in the row.

"I feel like the girls in the fairy tales who are led off to strange places and see fine things," said Effie, in a whisper, as they jingled through the gay streets.

"Ah, my deary, it *is* like a fairy tale, I do assure you, and you *will* see finer things than most children will tonight. Steady, now, and do just as I tell you, and don't say one word whatever you see," answered Nursey, quite quivering with excitement as she patted a large box in her lap, and nodded and laughed with twinkling eyes.

They drove into a dark yard, and Effie was led through a back door to a little room, where Nurse coolly proceeded to take off not only her cloak and hood, but her dress and shoes also. Effie stared and bit her lips, but kept still until out of the box came a little white fur coat and boots, a wreath of holly leaves and berries, and a candle with a frill of gold paper round it. A long "Oh!" escaped her then; and when she was dressed and saw herself in the glass, she started back, exclaiming, "Why, Nursey, I look like the spirit in my dream!"

"So you do; and that's the part you are to play, my pretty! Now whist, while I blind your eyes and put you in your place."

"Shall I be afraid?" whispered Effie, full of wonder; for as they went out she heard the sound of many voices, the tramp of many feet, and, in spite of the bandage, was sure a great light shone upon her when she stopped.

"You needn't be; I shall stand close by, and your ma will be there."

After the handkerchief was tied about her eyes, Nurse led Effie up some steps, and placed her on a high platform, where something like leaves touched her head, and the soft snap of lamps seemed to fill the air.

Music began as soon as Nurse clapped her hands, the voices outside sounded nearer, and the tramp was evidently coming up the stairs.

"Now, my precious, look and see how you and your dear ma have made a merry Christmas for them that needed it!"

Off went the bandage; and for a minute Effie really did think she was asleep again, for she actually stood in "a grove of Christmas trees," all gay and shining as in her vision. Twelve on a side, in two rows down the room, stood the little pines, each on its low table; and behind Effie a taller one rose to the roof, hung with wreaths of popcorn, apples, oranges, horns of candy, and cakes of all sorts, from sugary hearts to gingerbread Jumbos. On the smaller trees she saw many of her own discarded toys and those Nursey bought, as well as heaps that seemed to have rained down straight from that delightful Christmas country where she felt as if she was again.

"How splendid! Who is it for? What is that noise? Where is mamma?" cried Effie, pale with pleasure and surprise, as she stood looking down the brilliant little street from her high place.

Before Nurse could answer, the doors at the lower end flew open, and in marched twenty-four little blue-gowned orphan girls, singing sweetly, until amazement changed the song to cries of joy and wonder as the shining spectacle appeared. While they stood staring with round eyes at the wilderness of pretty things about them, mamma stepped up beside Effie, and holding her hand fast to give her courage, told the story of the dream in a few simple words, ending in this way:--

"So my little girl wanted to be a Christmas spirit too, and make this a happy day for those who had not as many pleasures and comforts as she has. She likes surprises, and we planned this for you all. She shall play the good fairy, and give each of you something from this tree, after which every one will find her own name on a small tree, and can go to enjoy it in her own way. March by, my dears, and let us fill your hands."

Nobody told them to do it, but all the hands were clapped heartily before a single child stirred; then one by one they came to look up wonderingly at the pretty giver of the feast as she leaned down to offer them great yellow oranges, red apples, bunches of grapes, bonbons, and cakes, till all were gone, and a double row of smiling faces turned toward her as the children filed back to their places in the orderly way they had been taught.

Then each was led to her own tree by the good ladies who had helped mamma with all their hearts; and the happy hubbub that arose would have satisfied even Santa Claus himself,--shrieks of joy, dances of delight, laughter and tears (for some tender little things could not bear so much pleasure at once, and sobbed with mouths full of candy and hands full of toys). How they ran to show one another the new treasures! how they peeped and tasted, pulled and pinched, until the air was full of queer noises, the floor covered with papers, and the little trees left bare of all but candles!

"I don't think heaven can be any gooder than this," sighed one small girl, as she looked about her in a blissful maze, holding her full apron with one hand, while she luxuriously carried sugarplums to her mouth with the other.

"Is that a truly angel up there?" asked another, fascinated by the little white figure with the wreath on its shining hair, who in some mysterious way had been the cause of all this merry-making.

"I wish I dared to go and kiss her for this splendid party," said a lame child, leaning on her crutch, as she stood near the steps, wondering how it seemed to sit in a mother's lap, as Effie was doing, while she watched the happy scene before her.

Effie heard her, and remembering Tiny Tim, ran down and put her arms about the pale child, kissing the wistful face, as she said sweetly, "You may; but mamma deserves the thanks. She did it all; I only dreamed about it."

Lame Katy felt as if "a truly angel" was embracing her, and could only stammer out her thanks, while the other children ran to see the pretty spirit, and touch her soft dress, until she stood in a crowd of blue gowns laughing as they held up their gifts for her to see and admire.

Mamma leaned down and whispered one word to the older girls; and suddenly they all took hands to dance round Effie, singing as they skipped.

It was a pretty sight, and the ladies found it hard to break up the happy revel; but it was late for small people, and too much fun is a mistake. So the girls fell into line, and marched before Effie and mamma again, to say goodnight with such grateful little faces that the eyes of those who looked grew dim with tears. Mamma kissed every one; and many a hungry childish heart felt as if the touch of those tender lips was their best gift. Effie shook so many small hands that her own tingled; and when Katy came she pressed a small doll into Effie's hand, whispering, "You didn't have a single present, and we had lots. Do keep that; it's the prettiest thing I got."

"I will," answered Effie, and held it fast until the last smiling face was gone, the surprise all over, and she safe in her own bed, too tired and happy for anything but sleep.

"Mamma, it was a beautiful surprise, and I thank you so much! I don't see how you did it; but I like it best of all the Christmases I ever had, and mean to make one every year. I had my splendid big present, and here is the dear little one to keep for love of poor Katy; so even that part of my wish came true."

And Effie fell asleep with a happy smile on her lips, her one humble gift still in her hand, and a new love for Christmas in her heart that never changed through a long life spent in doing good.

A MERRY CHRISTMAS
FROM LITTLE WOMEN

Jo was the first to wake in the gray dawn of Christmas morning. No stockings hung at the fireplace, and for a moment she felt as much disappointed as she did long ago, when her little sock fell down because it was crammed so full of goodies. Then she remembered her mother's promise and, slipping her hand under her pillow, drew out a little crimson-covered book. She knew it very well, for it was that beautiful old story of the best life ever lived, and Jo felt that it was a true guidebook for any pilgrim going on a long journey. She woke Meg with a "Merry Christmas," and bade her see what was under her pillow. A green-covered book appeared, with the same picture inside, and a few words written by their mother, which made their one present very precious in their eyes. Presently Beth and Amy woke to rummage and find their little books also, one dove-colored, the other blue, and all sat looking at and talking about them, while the east grew rosy with the coming day.

In spite of her small vanities, Margaret had a sweet and pious nature, which unconsciously influenced her sisters, especially Jo, who loved her very tenderly, and obeyed her because her advice was so gently given.

"Girls," said Meg seriously, looking from the tumbled head beside her to the two little night-capped ones in the room beyond, "Mother wants us to read and love and mind these books, and we must begin at once. We used to be faithful about it, but since Father went away and all this war trouble unsettled us, we have neglected many things. You can do as you please, but *I* shall keep my book on the table here and read a little every morning as soon as I wake, for I know it will do me good and help me through the day."

Then she opened her new book and began to read. Jo put her arm round her and, leaning cheek to cheek, read also, with the quiet expression so seldom seen on her restless face.

"How good Meg is! Come, Amy, let's do as they do. I'll help you with the hard words, and they'll explain things if we don't understand," whispered Beth, very much impressed by the pretty books and her sisters' example.

"I'm glad mine is blue," said Amy. and then the rooms were very still while the pages were softly turned, and the winter sunshine crept in to touch the bright heads and serious faces with a Christmas greeting.

"Where is Mother?" asked Meg, as she and Jo ran down to thank her for their gifts, half an hour later.

"Goodness only knows. Some poor creeter came a-beggin', and your ma went straight off to see what was needed. There never *was* such a woman for givin' away vittles and drink, clothes and firin'," replied Hannah, who had lived with the family since Meg was born, and was considered by them all more as a friend than a servant.

"She will be back soon, I think, so fry your cakes, and have everything ready," said Meg, looking over the presents which were collected in a basket and kept under the sofa, ready to be produced at the proper time. "Why, where is Amy's bottle of cologne?" she added, as the little flask did not appear.

"She took it out a minute ago, and went off with it to put a ribbon on it, or some such notion," replied Jo, dancing about the room to take the first stiffness off the new army slippers.

"How nice my handkerchiefs look, don't they? Hannah washed and ironed them for me, and I marked them all myself," said Beth, looking proudly at the somewhat uneven letters which had cost her such labor.

"Bless the child! She's gone and put 'Mother' on them instead of 'M. March'. How funny!" cried Jo, taking one up.

"Isn't that right? I thought it was better to do it so, because Meg's initials are M.M., and I don't want anyone to use these but Marmee," said Beth, looking troubled.

"It's all right, dear, and a very pretty idea, quite sensible too, for no one can ever mistake now. It will please her very much, I know," said Meg, with a frown for Jo and a smile for Beth.

"There's Mother. Hide the basket, quick!" cried Jo, as a door slammed and steps sounded in the hall.

Amy came in hastily, and looked rather abashed when she saw her sisters all waiting for her.

"Where have you been, and what are you hiding behind you?" asked Meg, surprised to see, by her hood and cloak, that lazy Amy had been out so early.

"Don't laugh at me, Jo! I didn't mean anyone should know till the time came. I only meant to change the little bottle for a big one, and I gave all my money to get it, and I'm truly trying not to be selfish any more."

As she spoke, Amy showed the handsome flask which replaced the cheap one, and looked so earnest and humble in her little effort to forget herself that Meg hugged her on the spot, and Jo pronounced her "a trump," while Beth ran to the window, and picked her finest rose to ornament the stately bottle.

"You see I felt ashamed of my present, after reading and talking about being good this morning, so I ran round the corner and changed it the minute I was up, and I'm *so* glad, for mine is the handsomest now."

Another bang of the street door sent the basket under the sofa, and the girls to the table, eager for breakfast.

"Merry Christmas, Marmee! Many of them! Thank you for our books. We read some, and mean to every day," they all cried in chorus.

"Merry Christmas, little daughters! I'm glad you began at once, and hope you will keep on. But I want to say one word before we sit down. Not far away from here lies a poor woman with a little newborn baby. Six children are huddled into one bed to keep from freezing, for they have no fire. There is nothing to eat over there, and the oldest boy came to tell me they were suffering hunger and cold. My girls, will you give them your breakfast as a Christmas present?"

They were all unusually hungry, having waited nearly an hour, and for a minute no one spoke, only a minute, for Jo exclaimed impetuously, "I'm so glad you came before we began!"

"May I go and help carry the things to the poor little children?" asked Beth eagerly.

"*I* shall take the cream and the muffings," added Amy, heroically giving up the article she most liked.

Meg was already covering the buckwheats, and piling the bread into one big plate.

"I thought you'd do it," said Mrs. March, smiling as if satisfied. "You shall all go and help me, and when we come back we will have bread and milk for breakfast, and make it up at dinnertime."

They were soon ready, and the procession set out. Fortunately it was early, and they went through back streets, so few people saw them, and no one laughed at the queer party.

A poor, bare, miserable room it was, with broken windows, no fire, ragged bedclothes, a sick mother, wailing baby, and a group of pale, hungry children cuddled under one old quilt, trying to keep warm.

How the big eyes stared and the blue lips smiled as the girls went in.

"Ach, mein Gott! It is good angels come to us!" said the poor woman, crying for joy.

"Funny angels in hoods and mittens," said Jo, and set them to laughing.

In a few minutes it really did seem as if kind spirits had been at work there. Hannah, who had carried wood, made a fire, and stopped up the broken panes with old hats and her own cloak. Mrs. March gave the mother tea and gruel, and comforted her with promises of help, while she dressed the little baby as tenderly as if it had been her own. The girls meantime spread the table, set the children round the fire, and fed them like so many hungry birds, laughing, talking, and trying to understand the funny broken English.

"Das ist gut!" "Die Engel-kinder!" cried the poor things as they ate and warmed their purple hands at the comfortable blaze. The girls had never been called angel children before, and thought it very agreeable, especially Jo, who had been considered a "Sancho" ever since she was born. That was a very happy breakfast, though they didn't get any of it. And when they went away, leaving comfort behind, I think there were not in all the city four merrier people than the hungry little girls who gave away their breakfasts and contented themselves with bread and milk on Christmas morning.

"That's loving our neighbor better than ourselves, and I like it," said Meg, as they set out their presents while their mother was upstairs collecting clothes for the poor Hummels.

Not a very splendid show, but there was a great deal of love done up in the few little bundles, and the tall vase of red roses, white chrysanthemums, and trailing vines, which stood in the middle, gave quite an elegant air to the table.

"She's coming! Strike up, Beth! Open the door, Amy! Three cheers for Marmee!" cried Jo, prancing about while Meg went to conduct Mother to the seat of honor.

Beth played her gayest march, Amy threw open the door, and Meg enacted escort with great dignity. Mrs. March was both surprised and touched, and smiled with her eyes full as she examined her presents and read the little notes which accompanied them. The slippers went on at once, a new handkerchief was slipped into her pocket, well scented with Amy's cologne, the rose was fastened in her bosom, and the nice gloves were pronounced a perfect fit.

There was a good deal of laughing and kissing and explaining, in the simple, loving fashion which makes these home festivals so pleasant at the time, so sweet to remember long afterward, and then all fell to work.

The morning charities and ceremonies took so much time that the rest of the day was devoted to preparations for the evening festivities. Being still too young to go often to the theater, and not rich enough to afford any great outlay for private performances, the girls put their wits to work, and necessity being the mother of invention, made whatever they needed. Very clever were some of their productions, pasteboard guitars, antique lamps made of old-fashioned butter boats covered with silver paper, gorgeous robes of old cotton, glittering with tin spangles from a pickle factory, and armor covered with the same useful diamond shaped bits left in sheets when the lids of preserve pots were cut out. The big chamber was the scene of many innocent revels.

No gentleman were admitted, so Jo played male parts to her heart's content and took immense satisfaction in a pair of russet leather boots given her by a friend, who knew a lady who knew an actor. These boots, an old foil, and a slashed doublet once used by an artist for some picture, were Jo's chief treasures and appeared on all occasions. The smallness of the company made it necessary for the two principal actors to take several parts apiece, and they certainly deserved some credit for the hard work they did in learning three or four different parts, whisking in and out of various costumes, and managing the stage besides. It was excellent drill for their memories, a harmless amusement, and employed many hours which otherwise would have been idle, lonely, or spent in less profitable society.

On Christmas night, a dozen girls piled onto the bed which was the dress circle, and sat before the blue and yellow chintz curtains in a most flattering state of expectancy. There was a good deal of rustling and whispering behind the curtain, a trifle of lamp smoke, and an occasional giggle from Amy, who was apt to get hysterical in the excitement of the moment. Presently a bell sounded, the curtains flew apart, and the *operatic tragedy* began.

"A gloomy wood," according to the one playbill, was represented by a few shrubs in pots, green baize on the floor, and a cave in the distance. This cave was made with a clothes horse for a roof, bureaus for walls, and in it was a small furnace in full blast, with a black pot on it and an old witch bending over it. The stage was dark and the glow of the furnace had a fine effect, especially as real steam issued from the kettle when the witch took off the cover. A moment was allowed for the first thrill to subside, then Hugo, the villain, stalked in with a clanking sword at his side, a slouching hat, black beard, mysterious cloak, and the boots. After pacing to and fro in much agitation, he struck his forehead, and burst out in a wild strain, singing of his hatred for Roderigo, his love for Zara, and his pleasing resolution to kill the one and win the other. The gruff tones of Hugo's voice, with an occasional shout when his feelings overcame him, were very impressive, and the audience applauded the moment he paused for breath. Bowing with the air of one accustomed to public praise, he stole to the cavern and ordered Hagar to come forth with a commanding, "What ho, minion! I need thee!"

Out came Meg, with gray horsehair hanging about her face, a red and black robe, a staff, and cabalistic signs upon her cloak. Hugo demanded a potion to make Zara adore him, and one to destroy Roderigo. Hagar, in a fine dramatic melody, promised both, and proceeded to call up the spirit who would bring the love philter.

Hither, hither, from thy home,
Airy sprite, I bid thee come!
Born of roses, fed on dew,
Charms and potions canst thou brew?
Bring me here, with elfin speed,
The fragrant philter which I need.
Make it sweet and swift and strong,
Spirit, answer now my song!

A soft strain of music sounded, and then at the back of the cave appeared a little figure in cloudy white, with glittering wings, golden hair, and a garland of roses on its head. Waving a wand, it sang...

Hither I come,
From my airy home,
Afar in the silver moon.
Take the magic spell,
And use it well,
Or its power will vanish soon!

And dropping a small, gilded bottle at the witch's feet, the spirit vanished. Another chant from Hagar produced another apparition, not a lovely one, for with a bang an ugly black imp appeared and, having croaked a reply, tossed a dark bottle at Hugo and disappeared with a mocking laugh. Having warbled his thanks and put the potions in his boots, Hugo departed, and Hagar informed the audience that as he had killed a few of her friends in times past, she had cursed him, and intends to thwart his plans, and be revenged on him. Then the curtain fell, and the audience reposed and ate candy while discussing the merits of the play.

A good deal of hammering went on before the curtain rose again, but when it became evident what a masterpiece of stage carpentery had been got up, no one murmured at the delay. It was truly superb. A tower rose to the ceiling, halfway up appeared a window with a lamp burning in it, and behind the white curtain appeared Zara in a lovely blue and silver dress, waiting for Roderigo. He came in gorgeous array, with plumed cap, red cloak, chestnut lovelocks, a guitar, and the boots, of course. Kneeling at the foot of the tower, he sang a serenade in melting tones. Zara replied and, after a musical dialogue, consented to fly. Then came the grand effect of the play. Roderigo produced a rope ladder, with five steps to it, threw up one end, and invited Zara to descend. Timidly she crept from her lattice, put her hand on Roderigo's shoulder, and was about to leap gracefully down when "Alas! Alas for Zara!" she forgot her train. It caught in the window, the tower tottered, leaned forward, fell with a crash, and buried the unhappy lovers in the ruins.

A universal shriek arose as the russet boots waved wildly from the wreck and a golden head emerged, exclaiming, "I told you so! I told you so!" With wonderful presence of mind, Don Pedro, the cruel sire, rushed in, dragged out his daughter, with a hasty aside...

"Don't laugh! Act as if it was all right!" and, ordering Roderigo up, banished him from the kingdom with wrath and scorn. Though decidedly shaken by the fall from the tower upon him, Roderigo defied the old gentleman and refused to stir. This dauntless example fired Zara. She also defied her sire, and he ordered them both to the deepest dungeons of the castle. A stout little retainer came in with chains and led them away, looking very much frightened and evidently forgetting the speech he ought to have made.

Act third was the castle hall, and here Hagar appeared, having come to free the lovers and finish Hugo. She hears him coming and hides, sees him put the potions into two cups of wine and bid the timid little servant, "Bear them to the captives in their cells, and tell them I shall come anon." The servant takes Hugo aside to tell him something, and Hagar changes the cups for two others which are harmless. Ferdinando, the "minion," carries them away, and Hagar puts back the cup which holds the poison meant for Roderigo.

Hugo, getting thirsty after a long warble, drinks it, loses his wits, and after a good deal of clutching and stamping, falls flat and dies, while Hagar informs him what she has done in a song of exquisite power and melody.

This was a truly thrilling scene, though some persons might have thought that the sudden tumbling down of a quantity of long red hair rather marred the effect of the villain's death. He was called before the curtain, and with great propriety appeared, leading Hagar, whose singing was considered more wonderful than all the rest of the performance put together.

Act fourth displayed the despairing Roderigo on the point of stabbing himself because he has been told that Zara has deserted him. Just as the dagger is at his heart, a lovely song is sung under his window, informing him that Zara is true but in danger, and he can save her if he will. A key is thrown in, which unlocks the door, and in a spasm of rapture he tears off his chains and rushes away to find and rescue his lady love.

Act fifth opened with a stormy scene between Zara and Don Pedro. He wishes her to go into a convent, but she won't hear of it, and after a touching appeal, is about to faint when Roderigo dashes in and demands her hand. Don Pedro refuses, because he is not rich. They shout and gesticulate tremendously but cannot agree, and Rodrigo is about to bear away the exhausted Zara, when the timid servant enters with a letter and a bag from Hagar, who has mysteriously disappeared. The latter informs the party that she bequeaths untold wealth to the young pair and an awful doom to Don Pedro, if he doesn't make them happy. The bag is opened, and several quarts of tin money shower down upon the stage till it is quite glorified with the glitter. This entirely softens the stern sire. He consents without a murmur, all join in a joyful chorus, and the curtain falls upon the lovers kneeling to receive Don Pedro's blessing in attitudes of the most romantic grace.

Tumultuous applause followed but received an unexpected check, for the cot bed, on which the dress circle was built, suddenly shut up and extinguished the enthusiastic audience. Roderigo and Don Pedro flew to the rescue, and all were taken out unhurt, though many were speechless with laughter. The excitement had hardly subsided when Hannah appeared, with "Mrs. March's compliments, and would the ladies walk down to supper."

This was a surprise even to the actors, and when they saw the table, they looked at one another in rapturous amazement. It was like Marmee to get up a little treat for them, but anything so fine as this was unheard of since the departed days of plenty. There was ice cream, actually two dishes of it, pink and white, and cake and fruit and distracting French bonbons and, in the middle of the table, four great bouquets of hot house flowers.

It quite took their breath away, and they stared first at the table and then at their mother, who looked as if she enjoyed it immensely.

"Is it fairies?" asked Amy.

"Santa Claus," said Beth.

"Mother did it." And Meg smiled her sweetest, in spite of her gray beard and white eyebrows.

"Aunt March had a good fit and sent the supper," cried Jo, with a sudden inspiration.

"All wrong. Old Mr. Laurence sent it," replied Mrs. March.

"The Laurence boy's grandfather! What in the world put such a thing into his head? We don't know him!" exclaimed Meg.

"Hannah told one of his servants about your breakfast party. He is an odd old gentleman, but that pleased him. He knew my father years ago, and he sent me a polite note this afternoon, saying he hoped I would allow him to express his friendly feeling toward my children by sending them a few trifles in honor of the day. I could not refuse, and so you have a little feast at night to make up for the bread-and-milk breakfast."

"That boy put it into his head, I know he did! He's a capital fellow, and I wish we could get acquainted. He looks as if he'd like to know us but he's bashful, and Meg is so prim she won't let me speak to him when we pass," said Jo, as the plates went round, and the ice began to melt out of sight, with ohs and ahs of satisfaction.

"You mean the people who live in the big house next door, don't you?" asked one of the girls. "My mother knows old Mr. Laurence, but says he's very proud and doesn't like to mix with his neighbors. He keeps his grandson shut up, when he isn't riding or walking with his tutor, and makes him study very hard. We invited him to our party, but he didn't come. Mother says he's very nice, though he never speaks to us girls."

"Our cat ran away once, and he brought her back, and we talked over the fence, and were getting on capitally, all about cricket, and so on, when he saw Meg coming, and walked off. I mean to know him some day, for he needs fun, I'm sure he does," said Jo decidedly.

"I like his manners, and he looks like a little gentleman, so I've no objection to your knowing him, if a proper opportunity comes. He brought the flowers himself, and I should have asked him in, if I had been sure what was going on upstairs. He looked so wistful as he went away, hearing the frolic and evidently having none of his own."

"It's a mercy you didn't, Mother!" laughed Jo, looking at her boots. "But we'll have another play sometime that he can see. Perhaps he'll help act. Wouldn't that be jolly?"

"I never had such a fine bouquet before! How pretty it is!" And Meg examined her flowers with great interest.

"They are lovely. But Beth's roses are sweeter to me," said Mrs. March, smelling the half-dead posy in her belt.

Beth nestled up to her, and whispered softly, "I wish I could send my bunch to Father. I'm afraid he isn't having such a merry Christmas as we are."

TESSA'S SURPRISES
FROM AUNT JO'S SCRAP-BAG, VOL. I

I.

Little Tessa sat alone by the fire, waiting for her father to come home from work. The children were fast asleep, all four in the big bed behind the curtain; the wind blew hard outside, and the snow beat on the window-panes; the room was large, and the fire so small and feeble that it didn't half warm the little bare toes peeping out of the old shoes on the hearth.

Tessa's father was an Italian plaster-worker, very poor, but kind and honest. The mother had died not long ago, and left twelve-year old Tessa to take care of the little children. She tried to be very wise and motherly, and worked for them like any little woman; but it was so hard to keep the small bodies warm and fed, and the small souls good and happy, that poor Tessa was often at her wits' end. She always waited for her father, no matter how tired she was, so that he might find his supper warm, a bit of fire, and a loving little face to welcome him. Tessa thought over her troubles at these quiet times, and made her plans; for her father left things to her a good deal, and she had no friends but Tommo, the harp-boy upstairs, and the lively cricket who lived in the chimney. To-night her face was very sober, and her pretty brown eyes very thoughtful as she stared at the fire and knit her brows, as if perplexed. She was not thinking of her old shoes, nor the empty closet, nor the boys' ragged clothes just then. No; she had a fine plan in her good little head, and was trying to discover how she could carry it out.

You see, Christmas was coming in a week; and she had set her heart on putting something in the children's stockings, as the mother used to do, for while she lived things were comfortable. Now Tessa had not a penny in the world, and didn't know how to get one, for all the father's earnings had to go for food, fire, and rent.

'If there were only fairies, ah! how heavenly that would be; for then I should tell them all I wish, and, pop! behold the fine things in my lap!' said Tessa to herself. 'I must earn the money; there is no one to give it to me, and I cannot beg. But what can I do, so small and stupid and shy as I am? I *must* find some way to give the little ones a nice Christmas. I *must*! I *must*!' and Tessa pulled her long hair, as if that would help her think.

But it didn't, and her heart got heavier and heavier; for it did seem hard that in a great city full of fine things, there should be none for poor Nono, Sep, and little Speranza. Just as Tessa's tears began to tumble off her eyelashes on to her brown cheeks, the cricket began to chirp. Of course, he didn't say a word; but it really did seem as if he had answered her question almost as well as a fairy; for, before he had piped a dozen shrill notes, an idea popped into Tessa's head—such a truly splendid idea that she clapped her hands and burst out laughing. 'I'll do it! I'll do it! if father will let me,' she said to herself, smiling and nodding at the fire. 'Tommo will like to have me go with him and sing, while he plays his harp in the streets. I know many songs, and may get money if I am not frightened; for people throw pennies to other little girls who only play the tambourine. Yes, I will try; and then, if I do well, the little ones shall have a Merry Christmas.'

So full of her plan was Tessa that she ran upstairs at once, and asked Tommo if he would take her with him on the morrow. Her friend was delighted, for he thought Tessa's songs very sweet, and was sure she would get money if she tried.

'But see, then, it is cold in the streets; the wind bites, and the snow freezes one's fingers. The day is very long, people are cross, and at night one is ready to die with weariness. Thou art so small, Tessa, I am afraid it will go badly with thee,' said Tommo, who was a merry, black-eyed boy of fourteen, with the kindest heart in the world under his old jacket.

'I do not mind cold and wet, and cross people, if I can get the pennies,' answered Tessa, feeling very brave with such a friend to help her. She thanked Tommo, and ran away to get ready, for she felt sure her father would not refuse her anything. She sewed up the holes in her shoes as well as she could, for she had much of that sort of cobbling to do; she mended her only gown, and laid ready the old hood and shawl which had been her mother's. Then she washed out little Ranza's frock and put it to dry, because she would not be able to do it the next day. She set the table and got things ready for breakfast, for Tommo went out early, and must not be kept waiting for her. She longed to make the beds and dress the children over night, she was in such a hurry to have all in order; but, as that could not be, she sat down again, and tried over all the songs she knew. Six pretty ones were chosen; and she sang away with all her heart in a fresh little voice so sweetly that the children smiled in their sleep, and her father's tired face brightened as he entered, for Tessa was his cheery cricket on the hearth. When she had told her plan, Peter Benari shook his head, and thought it would never do; but Tessa begged so hard, he consented at last that she should try it for one week, and sent her to bed the happiest little girl in New York.

Next morning the sun shone, but the cold wind blew, and the snow lay thick in the streets. As soon as her father was gone, Tessa flew about and put everything in nice order, telling the children she was going out for the day, and they were to mind Tommo's mother, who would see about the fire and the dinner; for the good woman loved Tessa, and entered into her little plans with all her heart. Nono and Giuseppe, or Sep, as they called him, wondered what she was going away for, and little Ranza cried at being left; but Tessa told them they would know all about it in a week, and have a fine time if they were good; so they kissed her all round and let her go.

Poor Tessa's heart beat fast as she trudged away with Tommo, who slung his harp over his shoulder, and gave her his hand. It was rather a dirty hand, but so kind that Tessa clung to it, and kept looking up at the friendly brown face for encouragement.

'We go first to the *café*, where many French and Italians eat the breakfast. They like my music, and often give me sips of hot coffee, which I like much. You too shall have the sips, and perhaps the pennies, for these people are greatly kind,' said Tommo, leading her into a large smoky place where many people sat at little tables, eating and drinking. 'See, now, have no fear; give them "Bella Monica;" that is merry and will make the laugh,' whispered Tommo, tuning his harp.

For a moment Tessa felt so frightened that she wanted to run away; but she remembered the empty stockings at home, and the fine plan, and she resolved *not* to give it up. One fat old Frenchman nodded to her, and it seemed to help her very much; for she began to sing before she thought, and that was the hardest part of it. Her voice trembled, and her cheeks grew redder and redder as she went on; but she kept her eyes fixed on her old shoes, and so got through without breaking down, which was very nice. The people laughed, for the song *was* merry; and the fat man smiled and nodded again. This gave her courage to try another, and she sung better and better each time; for Tommo played his best, and kept whispering to her, 'Yes; we go well; this is fine. They will give the money and the blessed coffee.'

So they did; for, when the little concert was over, several men put pennies in the cap Tessa offered, and the fat man took her on his knee, and ordered a mug of coffee, and some bread and butter for them both. This quite won her heart; and when they left the *café*, she kissed her hand to the old Frenchman, and said to her friend, 'How kind they are! I like this very much; and now it is not hard.'

But Tommo shook his curly head, and answered, soberly, 'Yes, I took you there first, for they love music, and are of our country; but up among the great houses we shall not always do well. The people there are busy or hard or idle, and care nothing for harps and songs. Do not skip and laugh too soon; for the day is long, and we have but twelve pennies yet.'

Tessa walked more quietly, and rubbed her cold hands, feeling that the world was a very big place, and wondering how the children got on at home without the little mother. Till noon they did not earn much, for every one seemed in a hurry, and the noise of many sleigh-bells drowned the music. Slowly they made their way up to the great squares where the big houses were, with fine ladies and pretty children at the windows. Here Tessa sung all her best songs, and Tommo played as fast as his fingers could fly; but it was too cold to have the windows open, so the pretty children could not listen long, and the ladies tossed out a little money, and soon went back to their own affairs.

All the afternoon the two friends wandered about, singing and playing, and gathering up their small harvest. At dusk they went home, Tessa so hoarse she could hardly speak, and so tired she fell asleep over her supper. But she had made half a dollar, for Tommo divided the money fairly, and she felt rich with her share. The other days were very much like this; sometimes they made more, sometimes less, but Tommo always 'went halves;' and Tessa kept on, in spite of cold and weariness, for her plans grew as her earnings increased, and now she hoped to get useful things, instead of candy and toys alone.

On the day before Christmas she made herself as tidy as she could, for she hoped to earn a good deal. She tied a bright scarlet handkerchief over the old hood, and the brilliant color set off her brown cheeks and bright eyes, as well as the pretty black braids of her hair. Tommo's mother lent her a pair of boots so big that they turned up at the toes, but there were no holes in them, and Tessa felt quite elegant in whole boots. Her hands were covered with chilblains, for she had no mittens; but she put them under her shawl, and scuffled merrily away in her big boots, feeling so glad that the week was over, and nearly three dollars safe in her pocket. How gay the streets were that day! how brisk every one was, and how bright the faces looked, as people trotted about with big baskets, holly-wreaths, and young evergreens going to blossom into splendid Christmas trees!

'If I could have a tree for the children, I'd never want anything again. But I can't; so I'll fill the socks all full, and be happy,' said Tessa, as she looked wistfully into the gay stores, and saw the heavy baskets go by.

'Who knows what may happen if we do well?' returned Tommo, nodding wisely, for he had a plan as well as Tessa, and kept chuckling over it as he trudged through the mud. They did *not* do well somehow, for every one seemed so full of their own affairs they could not stop to listen, even to 'Bella Monica,' but bustled away to spend their money in turkeys, toys, and trees. In the afternoon it began to rain, and poor Tessa's heart to fail her; for the big boots tired her feet, the cold wind made her hands ache, and the rain spoilt the fine red handkerchief. Even Tommo looked sober, and didn't whistle as he walked, for he also was disappointed, and his plan looked rather doubtful, the pennies came in so slowly.

'We'll try one more street, and then go home, thou art so tired, little one. Come; let me wipe thy face, and give me thy hand here in my jacket pocket; there it will be as warm as any kitten;' and kind Tommo brushed away the drops which were not *all* rain from Tessa's cheeks, tucked the poor hand into his ragged pocket, and led her carefully along the slippery streets, for the boots nearly tripped her up.

II.

At the first house, a cross old gentleman flapped his newspaper at them; at the second, a young gentleman and lady were so busy talking that they never turned their heads, and at the third, a servant came out and told them to go away, because some one was sick. At the fourth, some people let them sing all their songs and gave nothing. The next three houses were empty; and the last of all showed not a single face as they looked up anxiously. It was so cold, so dark and discouraging, that Tessa couldn't help one sob; and, as he glanced down at the little red nose and wet figure beside him, Tommo gave his harp an angry thump, and said something very fierce in Italian. They were just going to turn away; but they didn't, for that angry thump happened to be the best thing they could have done. All of a sudden a little head appeared at the window, as if the sound had brought it; then another and another, till there were five, of all heights and colors, and five eager faces peeped out, smiling and nodding to the two below.

'Sing, Tessa; sing! Quick! quick!' cried Tommo, twanging away with all his might, and showing his white teeth, as he smiled back at the little gentle-folk.

Bless us! How Tessa did tune up at that! She chirped away like a real bird, forgetting all about the tears on her cheeks, the ache in her hands, and the heaviness at her heart. The children laughed, and clapped their hands, and cried 'More! more! Sing another, little girl! Please do!' And away they went again, piping and playing, till Tessa's breath was gone, and Tommo's stout fingers tingled well.

'Mamma says, come to the door; it's too muddy to throw the money into the street!' cried out a kindly child's voice as Tessa held up the old cap, with beseeching eyes.

Up the wide stone steps went the street musicians, and the whole flock came running down to give a handful of silver, and ask all sorts of questions. Tessa felt so grateful that, without waiting for Tommo, she sang her sweetest little song all alone. It was about a lost lamb, and her heart was in the song; therefore she sang it well, so well that a pretty young lady came down to listen, and stood watching the bright-eyed girl, who looked about her as she sang, evidently enjoying the light and warmth of the fine hall, and the sight of the lovely children with their gay dresses, shining hair, and dainty little shoes.

'You have a charming voice, child. Who taught you to sing?' asked the young lady kindly.

'My mother. She is dead now; but I do not forget,' answered Tessa, in her pretty broken English.

'I wish she could sing at our tree, since Bella is ill,' cried one of the children peeping through the banisters.

'She is not fair enough for the angel, and too large to go up in the tree. But she sings sweetly, and looks as if she would like to see a tree,' said the young lady.

'Oh, so much!' exclaimed Tessa; adding eagerly, 'my sister Ranza is small and pretty as a baby-angel. She could sit up in the fine tree, and I could sing for her from under the table.'

'Sit down and warm yourself, and tell me about Ranza,' said the kind elder sister, who liked the confiding little girl, in spite of her shabby clothes.

So Tessa sat down and dried the big boots over the furnace, and told her story, while Tommo stood modestly in the background, and the children listened with faces full of interest.

'O Rose! let us see the little girl; and if she will do, let us have her, and Tessa can learn our song, and it will be splendid!' cried the biggest boy, who sat astride of a chair, and stared at the harp with round eyes.

'I'll ask mamma,' said Rose; and away she went into the dining-room close by. As the door opened, Tessa saw what looked to her like a fairy feast,—all silver mugs and flowery plates and oranges and nuts and rosy wine in tall glass pitchers, and smoking dishes that smelt so deliciously she could not restrain a little sniff of satisfaction.

'Are you hungry?' asked the boy, in a grand tone.

'Yes, sir,' meekly answered Tessa.

'I say, mamma; she wants something to eat. Can I give her an orange?' called the boy, prancing away into the splendid room, quite like a fairy prince, Tessa thought.

A plump motherly lady came out and looked at Tessa, asked a few questions, and then told her to come to-morrow with Ranza, and they would see what could be done. Tessa clapped her hands for joy,—she didn't mind the chilblains now,—and Tommo played a lively march, he was so pleased.

'Will you come, too, and bring your harp? You shall be paid, and shall have something from the tree, likewise,' said the motherly lady, who liked what Tessa gratefully told about his kindness to her.

'Ah, yes; I shall come with much gladness, and play as never in my life before,' cried Tommo, with a flourish of the old cap that made the children laugh.

'Give these to your brothers,' said the fairy prince, stuffing nuts and oranges into Tessa's hands.

'And these to the little girl,' added one of the young princesses, flying out of the dining-room with cakes and rosy apples for Ranza.

Tessa didn't know what to say; but her eyes were full, and she just took the mother's white hand in both her little grimy ones, and kissed it many times in her pretty Italian fashion. The lady understood her, and stroked her cheek softly, saying to her elder daughter, 'We must take care of this good little creature. Freddy, bring me your mittens; these poor hands must be covered. Alice, get your play-hood; this handkerchief is all wet; and, Maud, bring the old chinchilla tippet.'

The children ran, and in a minute there were lovely blue mittens on the red hands, a warm hood over the black braids, and a soft 'pussy' round the sore throat.

'Ah! so kind, so very kind! I have no way to say "thank you;" but Ranza shall be for you a heavenly angel, and I will sing my heart out for your tree!' cried Tessa, folding the mittens as if she would say a prayer of thankfulness if she knew how.

Then they went away, and the pretty children called after them, 'Come again, Tessa! come again, Tommo!' Now the rain didn't seem dismal, the wind cold, nor the way long, as they bought their gifts and hurried home, for kind words and the sweet magic of charity had changed all the world to them.

I think the good spirits who fly about on Christmas Eve, to help the loving fillers of little stockings, smiled very kindly on Tessa as she brooded joyfully over the small store of presents that seemed so magnificent to her. All the goodies were divided evenly into three parts and stowed away in father's three big socks, which hung against the curtain. With her three dollars, she had got a pair of shoes for Nono, a knit cap for Sep, and a pair of white stockings for Ranza; to her she also gave the new hood; to Nono the mittens; and to Sep the tippet.

'Now the dear boys can go out, and my Ranza will be ready for the lady to see, in her nice new things,' said Tessa, quite sighing with pleasure to see how well the gifts looked pinned up beside the bulging socks, which wouldn't hold them all. The little mother kept nothing for herself but the pleasure of giving everything away; yet, I think, she was both richer and happier than if she had kept them all. Her father laughed as he had not done since the mother died, when he saw how comically the old curtain had broken out into boots and hoods, stockings and tippets.

'I wish I had a gold gown and a silver hat for thee, my Tessa, thou art so good. May the saints bless and keep thee always!' said Peter Benari tenderly, as he held his little daughter close, and gave her the good-night kiss.

Tessa felt very rich as she crept under the faded counterpane, feeling as if she had received a lovely gift, and fell happily asleep with chubby Ranza in her arms, and the two rough black heads peeping out at the foot of the bed. She dreamed wonderful dreams that night, and woke in the morning to find real wonders before her eyes. She got up early, to see if the socks were all right, and there she found the most astonishing sight. Four socks, instead of three; and by the fourth, pinned out quite elegantly was a little dress, evidently meant for her—a warm, woollen dress, all made, and actually with bright buttons on it. It nearly took her breath away; so did the new boots on the floor, and the funny long stocking like a grey sausage, with a wooden doll staring out at the top, as if she said, politely, 'A Merry Christmas, ma'am!' Tessa screamed and danced in her delight, and up tumbled all the children to scream and dance with her, making a regular carnival on a small scale. Everybody hugged and kissed everybody else, offered sucks of orange, bites of cake, and exchanges of candy; every one tried on the new things, and pranced about in them like a flock of peacocks. Ranza skipped to and fro airily, dressed in her white socks and the red hood; the boys promenaded in their little shirts, one with his creaking new shoes and mittens, the other in his gay cap and fine tippet; and Tessa put her dress straight on, feeling that her father's 'gold gown' was not all a joke. In her long stocking she found all sorts of treasures; for Tommo had stuffed it full of queer things, and his mother had made gingerbread into every imaginable shape, from fat pigs to full omnibuses.

Dear me! What happy little souls they were that morning; and when they were quiet again, how like a fairy tale did Tessa's story sound to them. Ranza was quite ready to be an angel; and the boys promised to be marvellously good, if they were only allowed to see the tree at the 'palace,' as they called the great house.

Little Ranza was accepted with delight by the kind lady and her children, and Tessa learned the song quite easily. The boys *were* asked; and, after a happy day, the young Italians all returned, to play their parts at the fine Christmas party. Mamma and Miss Rose drilled them all; and when the folding-doors flew open, one rapturous 'Oh!' arose from the crowd of children gathered to the festival. I assure you, it was splendid; the great tree glittering with lights and gifts; and, on her invisible perch, up among the green boughs, sat the little golden-haired angel, all in white, with downy wings, a shining crown on her head, and the most serene satisfaction in her blue eyes, as she stretched her chubby arms to those below, and smiled her baby smile at them. Before any one could speak, a voice, as fresh and sweet as a lark's, sang the Christmas Carol so blithely that every one stood still to hear, and then clapped till the little angel shook on her perch, and cried out, 'Be 'till, or me'll fall!' How they laughed at that; and what fun they had talking to Ranza, while Miss Rose stripped the tree, for the angel could not resist temptation, and amused herself by eating all the bonbons she could reach, till she was taken down, to dance about like a fairy in a white frock and red shoes. Tessa and her friends had many presents; the boys were perfect lambs, Tommo played for the little folks to dance, and every one said something friendly to the strangers, so that they did not feel shy, in spite of shabby clothes. It was a happy night: and all their lives they remembered it as something too beautiful and bright to be quite true. Before they went home, the kind mamma told Tessa she should be her friend, and gave her a motherly kiss, which warmed the child's heart and seemed to set a seal upon that promise. It was faithfully kept, for the rich lady had been touched by Tessa's patient struggles and sacrifices; and for many years, thanks to her benevolence, there was no end to Tessa's Surprises.

TILLY'S CHRISTMAS
FROM AUNT JO'S SCRAP-BAG, VOL. I

'I'm so glad to-morrow is Christmas, because I'm going to have lots of presents.'

'So am I glad, though I don't expect any presents but a pair of mittens.'

'And so am I; but I shan't have any presents at all.'

As the three little girls trudged home from school they said these things, and as Tilly spoke, both the others looked at her with pity and some surprise, for she spoke cheerfully, and they wondered how she could be happy when she was so poor she could have no presents on Christmas.

'Don't you wish you could find a purse full of money right here in the path?' said Kate, the child who was going to have 'lots of presents.'

'Oh, don't I, if I could keep it honestly!' and Tilly's eyes shone at the very thought.

'What would you buy?' asked Bessy, rubbing her cold hands, and longing for her mittens.

'I'd buy a pair of large, warm blankets, a load of wood, a shawl for mother, and a pair of shoes for me; and if there was enough left,

I'd give Bessy a new hat, and then she needn't wear Ben's old felt one,' answered Tilly.

The girls laughed at that; but Bessy pulled the funny hat over her ears, and said she was much obliged but she'd rather have candy.

'Let's look, and maybe we *can* find a purse. People are always going about with money at Christmas time, and some one may lose it here,' said Kate.

So, as they went along the snowy road, they looked about them, half in earnest, half in fun. Suddenly Tilly sprang forward, exclaiming,—

'I see it! I've found it!'

The others followed, but all stopped disappointed; for it wasn't a purse, it was only a little bird. It lay upon the snow with its wings spread and feebly fluttering, as if too weak to fly. Its little feet were benumbed with cold; its once bright eyes were dull with pain, and instead of a blithe song, it could only utter a faint chirp, now and then, as if crying for help.

'Nothing but a stupid old robin; how provoking!' cried Kate, sitting down to rest.

'I shan't touch it. I found one once, and took care of it, and the ungrateful thing flew away the minute it was well,' said Bessy, creeping under Kate's shawl, and putting her hands under her chin to warm them.

'Poor little birdie! How pitiful he looks, and how glad he must be to see some one coming to help him! I'll take him up gently, and carry him home to mother. Don't be frightened, dear, I'm your friend;' and Tilly knelt down in the snow, stretching her hand to the bird, with the tenderest pity in her face.

Kate and Bessy laughed.

'Don't stop for that thing; it's getting late and cold: let's go on and look for the purse,' they said moving away.

'You wouldn't leave it to die!' cried Tilly. 'I'd rather have the bird than the money, so I shan't look any more. The purse wouldn't be mine, and I should only be tempted to keep it; but this poor thing will thank and love me, and I'm *so* glad I came in time.'

Gently lifting the bird, Tilly felt its tiny cold claws cling to her hand, and saw its dim eyes brighten as it nestled down with a grateful chirp.

'Now I've got a Christmas present after all,' she said, smiling, as they walked on. 'I always wanted a bird, and this one will be such a pretty pet for me.'

'He'll fly away the first chance he gets, and die anyhow; so you'd better not waste your time over him,' said Bessy.

'He can't pay you for taking care of him, and my mother says it isn't worth while to help folks that can't help us,' added Kate.

'My mother says, "Do as you'd be done by;" and I'm sure I'd like any one to help me if I was dying of cold and hunger. "Love your neighbour as yourself," is another of her sayings. This bird is my little neighbour, and I'll love him and care for him, as I often wish our rich neighbour would love and care for us,' answered Tilly, breathing her warm breath over the benumbed bird, who looked up at her with confiding eyes, quick to feel and know a friend.

'What a funny girl you are,' said Kate; 'caring for that silly bird, and talking about loving your neighbour in that sober way. Mr. King don't care a bit for you, and never will, though he knows how poor you are; so I don't think your plan amounts to much.'

'I believe it, though; and shall do my part, any way. Good-night. I hope you'll have a merry Christmas, and lots of pretty things,' answered Tilly, as they parted.

Her eyes were full, and she felt so poor as she went on alone toward the little old house where she lived. It would have been so pleasant to know that she was going to have some of the pretty things all children love to find in their full stockings on Christmas morning. And pleasanter still to have been able to give her mother something nice. So many comforts were needed, and there was no hope of getting them; for they could barely get food and fire.

'Never mind, birdie, we'll make the best of what we have, and be merry in spite of every thing. *You* shall have a happy Christmas, any way; and I know God won't forget us if every one else does.'

She stopped a minute to wipe her eyes, and lean her cheek against the bird's soft breast, finding great comfort in the little creature, though it could only love her, nothing more.

'See, mother, what a nice present I've found,' she cried, going in with a cheery face that was like sunshine in the dark room.

'I'm glad of that, dearie; for I haven't been able to get my little girl anything but a rosy apple. Poor bird! Give it some of your warm bread and milk.'

'Why, mother, what a big bowlful! I'm afraid you gave me all the milk,' said Tilly, smiling over the nice, steaming supper that stood ready for her.

'I've had plenty, dear. Sit down and dry your wet feet, and put the bird in my basket on this warm flannel.'

Tilly peeped into the closet and saw nothing there but dry bread.

'Mother's given me all the milk, and is going without her tea, 'cause she knows I'm hungry. Now I'll surprise her, and she shall have a good supper too. She is going to split wood, and I'll fix it while she's gone.'

So Tilly put down the old tea-pot, carefully poured out a part of the milk, and from her pocket produced a great, plummy bun, that one of the school-children had given her, and she had saved for her mother. A slice of the dry bread was nicely toasted, and the bit of butter set by for her put on it. When her mother came in there was the table drawn up in a warm place, a hot cup of tea ready, and Tilly and birdie waiting for her.

Such a poor little supper, and yet such a happy one; for love, charity, and contentment were guests there, and that Christmas eve was a blither one than that up at the great house, where lights shone, fires blazed, a great tree glittered, and music sounded, as the children danced and played.

'We must go to bed early, for we've only wood enough to last over to-morrow. I shall be paid for my work the day after, and then we can get some,' said Tilly's mother, as they sat by the fire.

'If my bird was only a fairy bird, and would give us three wishes, how nice it would be! Poor dear, he can't give me any thing; but it's no matter,' answered Tilly, looking at the robin, who lay in the basket with his head under his wing, a mere little feathery bunch.

'He can give you one thing, Tilly,—the pleasure of doing good. That is one of the sweetest things in life; and the poor can enjoy it as well as the rich.'

As her mother spoke, with her tired hand softly stroking her little daughter's hair, Tilly suddenly started and pointed to the window, saying, in a frightened whisper,—

'I saw a face,—a man's face, looking in! It's gone now; but I truly saw it.'

'Some traveller attracted by the light perhaps. I'll go and see.' And Tilly's mother went to the door.

No one was there. The wind blew cold, the stars shone, the snow lay white on field and wood, and the Christmas moon was glittering in the sky.

'What sort of a face was it?' asked Tilly's mother, coming back.

'A pleasant sort of face, I think; but I was so startled I don't quite know what it was like. I wish we had a curtain there,' said Tilly.

'I like to have our light shine out in the evening, for the road is dark and lonely just here, and the twinkle of our lamp is pleasant to people's eyes as they go by. We can do so little for our neighbours, I am glad to cheer the way for them. Now put these poor old shoes to dry, and go to bed, dearie; I'll come soon.'

Tilly went, taking her bird with her to sleep in his basket near by, lest he should be lonely in the night.

Soon the little house was dark and still, and no one saw the Christmas spirits at their work that night.

When Tilly opened the door next morning, she gave a loud cry, clapped her hands, and then stood still; quite speechless with wonder and delight. There, before the door, lay a great pile of wood, all ready to burn, a big bundle and a basket, with a lovely nosegay of winter roses, holly, and evergreen tied to the handle.

'Oh, mother! did the fairies do it?' cried Tilly, pale with her happiness, as she seized the basket, while her mother took in the bundle.

'Yes, dear, the best and dearest fairy in the world, called "Charity." She walks abroad at Christmas time, does beautiful deeds like this, and does not stay to be thanked,' answered her mother with full eyes, as she undid the parcel.

There they were,—the warm, thick blankets, the comfortable shawls, the new shoes, and, best of all, a pretty winter hat for Bessy. The basket was full of good things to eat, and on the flowers lay a paper, saying,—

'For the little girl who loves her neighbour as herself.'

'Mother, I really think my bird is a fairy bird, and all these splendid things come from him,' said Tilly, laughing and crying with joy.

It really did seem so, for as she spoke, the robin flew to the table, hopped to the nosegay, and perching among the roses, began to chirp with all his little might. The sun streamed in on flowers, bird, and happy child, and no one saw a shadow glide away from the window; no one ever knew that Mr. King had seen and heard the little girls the night before, or dreamed that the rich neighbour had learned a lesson from the poor neighbour.

And Tilly's bird *was* a fairy bird; for by her love and tenderness to the helpless thing, she brought good gifts to herself, happiness to the unknown giver of them, and a faithful little friend who did not fly away, but stayed with her till the snow was gone, making summer for her in the winter-time.

A COUNTRY CHRISTMAS
FROM PROVERB TALES

"A handful of good life is worth a bushel of learning."

"DEAR EMILY,—I have a brilliant idea, and at once hasten to share it with you. Three weeks ago I came up here to the wilds of Vermont to visit my old aunt, also to get a little quiet and distance in which to survey certain new prospects which have opened before me, and to decide whether I will marry a millionaire and become a queen of society, or remain 'the charming Miss Vaughan' and wait till the conquering hero comes.

"Aunt Plumy begs me to stay over Christmas, and I have consented, as I always dread the formal dinner with which my guardian celebrates the day.

"My brilliant idea is this. I'm going to make it a real old-fashioned frolic, and won't you come and help me? You will enjoy it immensely I am sure, for Aunt is a character, Cousin Saul worth seeing, and Ruth a far prettier girl than any of the city rose-buds coming out this season. Bring Leonard Randal along with you to take notes for his new book; then it will be fresher and truer than the last, clever as it was.

"The air is delicious up here, society amusing, this old farmhouse full of treasures, and your bosom friend pining to embrace you. Just telegraph yes or no, and we will expect you on Tuesday.

"Ever yours,
"Sophie Vaughan."

"They will both come, for they are as tired of city life and as fond of change as I am," said the writer of the above, as she folded her letter and went to get it posted without delay.

Aunt Plumy was in the great kitchen making pies; a jolly old soul, with a face as ruddy as a winter apple, a cheery voice, and the kindest heart that ever beat under a gingham gown. Pretty Ruth was chopping the mince, and singing so gaily as she worked that the four-and-twenty immortal blackbirds could not have put more music into a pie than she did. Saul was piling wood into the big oven, and Sophie paused a moment on the threshold to look at him, for she always enjoyed the sight of this stalwart cousin, whom she likened to a Norse viking, with his fair hair and beard, keen blue eyes, and six feet of manly height, with shoulders that looked broad and strong enough to bear any burden.

His back was toward her, but he saw her first, and turned his flushed face to meet her, with the sudden lighting up it always showed when she approached.

"I've done it, Aunt; and now I want Saul to post the letter, so we can get a speedy answer."

"Just as soon as I can hitch up, cousin;" and Saul pitched in his last log, looking ready to put a girdle round the earth in less than forty minutes.

"Well, dear, I ain't the least mite of objection, as long as it pleases you. I guess we can stan' it ef your city folks can. I presume to say things will look kind of sing'lar to 'em, but I s'pose that's what they come for. Idle folks do dreadful queer things to amuse 'em;" and Aunt Plumy leaned on the rolling-pin to smile and nod with a shrewd twinkle of her eye, as if she enjoyed the prospect as much as Sophie did.

"I shall be afraid of 'em, but I'll try not to make you ashamed of me," said Ruth, who loved her charming cousin even more than she admired her.

"No fear of that, dear. They will be the awkward ones, and you must set them at ease by just being your simple selves, and treating them as if they were everyday people. Nell is very nice and jolly when she drops her city ways, as she must here. She will enter into the spirit of the fun at once, and I know you'll all like her. Mr. Randal is rather the worse for too much praise and petting, as successful people are apt to be, so a little plain talk and rough work will do him good. He is a true gentleman in spite of his airs and elegance, and he will take it all in good part, if you treat him like a man and not a lion."

"I'll see to him," said Saul, who had listened with great interest to the latter part of Sophie's speech, evidently suspecting a lover, and enjoying the idea of supplying him with a liberal amount of "plain talk and rough work."

"I'll keep 'em busy if that's what they need, for there will be a sight to do, and we can't get help easy up here. Our darters don't hire out much. Work to home till they marry, and don't go gaddin' 'round gettin' their heads full of foolish notions, and forgettin' all the useful things their mothers taught 'em."

Aunt Plumy glanced at Ruth as she spoke, and a sudden color in the girl's cheeks proved that the words hit certain ambitious fancies of this pretty daughter of the house of Basset.

"They shall do their parts and not be a trouble; I'll see to that, for you certainly are the dearest aunt in the world to let me take possession of you and yours in this way," cried Sophie, embracing the old lady with warmth.

Saul wished the embrace could be returned by proxy, as his mother's hands were too floury to do more than hover affectionately round the delicate face that looked so fresh and young beside her wrinkled one. As it could not be done, he fled temptation and "hitched up" without delay.

The three women laid their heads together in his absence, and Sophie's plan grew apace, for Ruth longed to see a real novelist and a fine lady, and Aunt Plumy, having plans of her own to further, said "Yes, dear," to every suggestion.

Great was the arranging and adorning that went on that day in the old farmhouse, for Sophie wanted her friends to enjoy this taste of country pleasures, and knew just what additions would be indispensable to their comfort; what simple ornaments would be in keeping with the rustic stage on which she meant to play the part of prima donna.

Next day a telegram arrived accepting the invitation, for both the lady and the lion. They would arrive that afternoon, as little preparation was needed for this impromptu journey, the novelty of which was its chief charm to these *blasé* people.

Saul wanted to get out the double sleigh and span, for he prided himself on his horses, and a fall of snow came most opportunely to beautify the landscape and add a new pleasure to Christmas festivities.

But Sophie declared that the old yellow sleigh, with Punch, the farm-horse, must be used, as she wished everything to be in keeping; and Saul obeyed, thinking he had never seen anything prettier than his cousin when she appeared in his mother's old-fashioned camlet cloak and blue silk pumpkin hood. He looked remarkably well himself in his fur coat, with hair and beard brushed till they shone like spun gold, a fresh color in his cheek, and the sparkle of amusement in his eyes, while excitement gave his usually grave face the animation it needed to be handsome.

Away they jogged in the creaking old sleigh, leaving Ruth to make herself pretty, with a fluttering heart, and Aunt Plumy to dish up a late dinner fit to tempt the most fastidious appetite.

"She has not come for us, and there is not even a stage to take us up. There must be some mistake," said Emily Herrick, as she looked about the shabby little station where they were set down.

"That is the never-to-be-forgotten face of our fair friend, but the bonnet of her grandmother, if my eyes do not deceive me," answered Randal, turning to survey the couple approaching in the rear.

"Sophie Vaughan, what do you mean by making such a guy of yourself?" exclaimed Emily, as she kissed the smiling face in the hood and stared at the quaint cloak.

"I'm dressed for my part, and I intend to keep it up. This is our host, my cousin, Saul Basset. Come to the sleigh at once, he will see to your luggage," said Sophie, painfully conscious of the antiquity of her array as her eyes rested on Emily's pretty hat and mantle, and the masculine elegance of Randal's wraps.

They were hardly tucked in when Saul appeared with a valise in one hand and a large trunk on his shoulder, swinging both on to a wood-sled that stood near by as easily as if they had been hand-bags.

"That is your hero, is it? Well, he looks it, calm and comely, taciturn and tall," said Emily, in a tone of approbation.

"He should have been named Samson or Goliath; though I believe it was the small man who slung things about and turned out the hero in the end," added Randal, surveying the performance with interest and a touch of envy, for much pen work had made his own hands as delicate as a woman's.

"Saul doesn't live in a glass house, so stones won't hurt him. Remember sarcasm is forbidden and sincerity the order of the day. You are country folks now, and it will do you good to try their simple, honest ways for a few days."

Sophie had no time to say more, for Saul came up and drove off with the brief remark that the baggage would "be along right away."

Being hungry, cold and tired, the guests were rather silent during the short drive, but Aunt Plumy's hospitable welcome, and the savory fumes of the dinner awaiting them, thawed the ice and won their hearts at once.

"Isn't it nice? Aren't you glad you came?" asked Sophie, as she led her friends into the parlor, which she had redeemed from its primness by putting bright chintz curtains to the windows, hemlock boughs over the old portraits, a china bowl of flowers on the table, and a splendid fire on the wide hearth.

"It is perfectly jolly, and this is the way I begin to enjoy myself," answered Emily, sitting down upon the home-made rug, whose red flannel roses bloomed in a blue list basket.

"If I may add a little smoke to your glorious fire, it will be quite perfect. Won't Samson join me?" asked Randal, waiting for permission, cigar-case in hand.

"He has no small vices, but you may indulge yours," answered Sophie, from the depths of a grandmotherly chair.

Emily glanced up at her friend as if she caught a new tone in her voice, then turned to the fire again with a wise little nod, as if confiding some secret to the reflection of herself in the bright brass andiron.

"His Delilah does not take this form. I wait with interest to discover if he has one. What a daisy the sister is. Does she ever speak?" asked Randal, trying to lounge on the haircloth sofa, where he was slipping uncomfortably about.

"Oh yes, and sings like a bird. You shall hear her when she gets over her shyness. But no trifling, mind you, for it is a jealously guarded daisy and not to be picked by any idle hand," said Sophie warningly, as she recalled Ruth's blushes and Randal's compliments at dinner.

"I should expect to be annihilated by the big brother if I attempted any but the 'sincerest' admiration and respect. Have no fears on that score, but tell us what is to follow this superb dinner. An apple bee, spinning match, husking party, or primitive pastime of some sort, I have no doubt."

"As you are new to our ways I am going to let you rest this

evening. We will sit about the fire and tell stories. Aunt is a master hand at that, and Saul has reminiscences of the war that are well worth hearing if we can only get him to tell them."

"Ah, he was there, was he?"

"Yes, all through it, and is Major Basset, though he likes his plain name best. He fought splendidly and had several wounds, though only a mere boy when he earned his scars and bars. I'm very proud of him for that," and Sophie looked so as she glanced at the photograph of a stripling in uniform set in the place of honor on the high mantel-piece.

"We must stir him up and hear these martial memories. I want some new incidents, and shall book all I can get, if I may."

Here Randal was interrupted by Saul himself, who came in with an armful of wood for the fire.

"Anything more I can do for you, cousin?" he asked, surveying the scene with a rather wistful look.

"Only come and sit with us and talk over war times with Mr. Randal."

"When I've foddered the cattle and done my chores I'd be pleased to. What regiment were you in?" asked Saul, looking down from his lofty height upon the slender gentleman, who answered briefly,—

"In none. I was abroad at the time."

"Sick?"

"No, busy with a novel."

"Took four years to write it?"

"I was obliged to travel and study before I could finish it. These things take more time to work up than outsiders would believe."

"Seems to me our war was a finer story than any you could find in Europe, and the best way to study it would be to fight it out. If you want heroes and heroines you'd have found plenty of 'em there."

"I have no doubt of it, and shall be glad to atone for my seeming neglect of them by hearing about your own exploits, Major."

Randal hoped to turn the conversation gracefully; but Saul was not to be caught, and left the room, saying, with a gleam of fun in his eye,—

"I can't stop now; heroes can wait, pigs can't."

The girls laughed at this sudden descent from the sublime to the ridiculous, and Randal joined them, feeling his condescension had not been unobserved.

As if drawn by the merry sound Aunt Plumy appeared, and being established in the rocking-chair fell to talking as easily as if she had known her guests for years.

"Laugh away, young folks, that's better for digestion than any of the messes people use. Are you troubled with dyspepsy, dear? You didn't seem to take your vittles very hearty, so I mistrusted you was delicate," she said, looking at Emily, whose pale cheeks and weary eyes told the story of late hours and a gay life.

"I haven't eaten so much for years, I assure you, Mrs. Basset; but it was impossible to taste all your good things. I am not dyspeptic, thank you, but a little seedy and tired, for I've been working rather hard lately."

"Be you a teacher? or have you a 'perfessun,' as they call a trade nowadays?" asked the old lady in a tone of kindly interest, which prevented a laugh at the idea of Emily's being anything but a beauty and a belle. The others kept their countenances with difficulty, and she answered demurely,—

"I have no trade as yet, but I dare say I should be happier if I had."

"Not a doubt on't, my dear."

"What would you recommend, ma'am?"

"I should say dressmakin' was rather in your line, ain't it. Your clothes is dreadful tasty, and do you credit if you made 'em yourself," and Aunt Plumy surveyed with feminine interest the simple elegance of the travelling dress which was the masterpiece of a French modiste.

"No, ma'am, I don't make my own things, I'm too lazy. It takes so much time and trouble to select them that I have only strength left to wear them."

"Housekeepin' used to be the favorite perfessun in my day. It ain't fashionable now, but it needs a sight of trainin' to be perfect in all that's required, and I've an idee it would be a sight healthier and usefuller than the paintin' and music and fancy work young women do nowadays."

"But every one wants some beauty in their lives, and each one has a different sphere to fill, if one can only find it."

"'Pears to me there's no call for so much art when nater is full of beauty for them that can see and love it. As for 'spears' and so on, I've a notion if each of us did up our own little chores smart and thorough we needn't go wanderin' round to set the world to rights. That's the Lord's job, and I presume to say He can do it without any advice of ourn."

Something in the homely but true words seemed to rebuke the three listeners for wasted lives, and for a moment there was no sound but the crackle of the fire, the brisk click of the old lady's knitting needles, and Ruth's voice singing overhead as she made ready to join the party below.

"To judge by that sweet sound you have done one of your 'chores' very beautifully, Mrs. Basset, and in spite of the follies of our day, succeeded in keeping one girl healthy, happy and unspoiled," said Emily, looking up into the peaceful old face with her own lovely one full of respect and envy.

"I do hope so, for she's my ewe lamb, the last of four dear little girls; all the rest are in the burying ground 'side of father. I don't expect to keep her long, and don't ought to regret when I lose her, for Saul is the best of sons; but daughters is more to mothers somehow, and I always yearn over girls that is left without a broodin' wing to keep 'em safe and warm in this world of tribulation."

Aunt Plumy laid her hand on Sophie's head as she spoke, with such a motherly look that both girls drew nearer, and Randal resolved to put her in a book without delay.

Presently Saul returned with little Ruth hanging on his arm and shyly nestling near him as he took the three-cornered leathern chair in the chimney nook, while she sat on a stool close by.

"Now the circle is complete and the picture perfect. Don't light the lamps yet, please, but talk away and let me make a mental study of you. I seldom find so charming a scene to paint," said Randal, beginning to enjoy himself immensely, with a true artist's taste for novelty and effect.

"Tell us about your book, for we have been reading it as it comes out in the magazine, and are much exercised about how it's going to end," began Saul, gallantly throwing himself into the breach, for a momentary embarrassment fell upon the women at the idea of sitting for their portraits before they were ready.

"Do you really read my poor serial up here, and do me the honor to like it?" asked the novelist, both flattered and amused, for his work was of the æsthetic sort, microscopic studies of character, and careful pictures of modern life.

"Sakes alive, why shouldn't we," cried Aunt Plumy. "We have some eddication, though we ain't very genteel. We've got a town libry, kep up by the women mostly, with fairs and tea parties and so on. We have all the magazines reg'lar, and Saul reads out the pieces while Ruth sews and I knit, my eyes bein' poor. Our winter is long and evenins would be kinder lonesome if we didn't have novils and newspapers to cheer 'em up."

"I am very glad I can help to beguile them for you. Now tell me what you honestly think of my work? Criticism is always valuable, and I should really like yours, Mrs. Basset," said Randal, wondering what the good woman would make of the delicate analysis and worldly wisdom on which he prided himself.

Short work, as Aunt Plumy soon showed him, for she rather enjoyed freeing her mind at all times, and decidedly resented the insinuation that country folk could not appreciate light literature as well as city people.

"I ain't no great of a jedge about anything but nat'ralness of books, and it really does seem as if some of your men and women was dreadful uncomfortable creaters. 'Pears to me it ain't wise to be always pickin' ourselves to pieces and pryin' into things that ought to come gradual by way of experience and the visitations of Providence. Flowers won't blow worth a cent ef you pull 'em open. Better wait and see what they can do alone. I do relish the smart sayins, the odd ways of furrin parts, and the sarcastic slaps at folkses weak spots. But, massy knows, we can't live on spice-cake and Charlotte Ruche, and I do feel as if books was more sustainin' ef they was full of every-day people and things, like good bread and butter. Them that goes to the heart and ain't soon forgotten is the kind I hanker for. Mis Terry's books now, and Mis Stowe's, and Dickens's Christmas pieces,—them is real sweet and cheerin', to my mind."

As the blunt old lady paused it was evident she had produced a sensation, for Saul smiled at the fire, Ruth looked dismayed at this assault upon one of her idols, and the young ladies were both astonished and amused at the keenness of the new critic who dared express what they had often felt. Randal, however, was quite composed and laughed good-naturedly, though secretly feeling as if a pail of cold water had been poured over him.

"Many thanks, madam; you have discovered my weak point with surprising accuracy. But you see I cannot help 'picking folks to pieces,' as you have expressed it; that is my gift, and it has its attractions, as the sale of my books will testify. People like the 'spice-bread,' and as that is the only sort my oven will bake, I must keep on in order to make my living."

"So rumsellers say, but it ain't a good trade to foller, and I'd chop wood 'fore I'd earn my livin' harmin' my feller man. 'Pears to me I'd let my oven cool a spell, and hunt up some homely, happy folks to write about; folks that don't borrer trouble and go lookin' for holes in their neighbors' coats, but take their lives brave and cheerful; and rememberin' we are all human, have pity on the weak, and try to be as full of mercy, patience and lovin' kindness as Him who made us. That sort of a book would do a heap of good; be real warmin' and strengthenin', and make them that read it love the man that wrote it, and remember him when he was dead and gone."

"I wish I could!" and Randal meant what he said, for he was as tired of his own style, as a watch-maker might be of the magnifying glass through which he strains his eyes all day. He knew that the heart was left out of his work, and that both mind and soul were growing morbid with dwelling on the faulty, absurd and metaphysical phases of life and character. He often threw down his pen and vowed he would write no more; but he loved ease and the books brought money readily; he was accustomed to the stimulant of praise and missed it as the toper misses his wine, so that which had once been a pleasure to himself and others was fast becoming a burden and a disappointment.

The brief pause which followed his involuntary betrayal of discontent was broken by Ruth, who exclaimed, with a girlish enthusiasm that overpowered girlish bashfulness,—

"*I* think all the novels are splendid! I hope you will write hundreds more, and I shall live to read 'em."

"Bravo, my gentle champion! I promise that I will write one more at least, and have a heroine in it whom your mother will both admire and love," answered Randal, surprised to find how grateful he was for the girl's approval, and how rapidly his trained fancy began to paint the background on which he hoped to copy this fresh, human daisy.

Abashed by her involuntary outburst, Ruth tried to efface herself behind Saul's broad shoulder, and he brought the conversation back to its starting-point by saying in a tone of the most sincere interest,—

"Speaking of the serial, I am very anxious to know how your hero comes out. He is a fine fellow, and I can't decide whether he is going to spoil his life marrying that silly woman, or do something grand and generous, and not be made a fool of."

"Upon my soul, I don't know myself. It is very hard to find new finales. Can't you suggest something, Major? then I shall not be obliged to leave my story without an end, as people complain I am rather fond of doing."

"Well, no, I don't think I've anything to offer. Seems to me it isn't the sensational exploits that show the hero best, but some great sacrifice quietly made by a common sort of man who is noble without knowing it. I saw a good many such during the war, and often wish I could write them down, for it is surprising how much courage, goodness and real piety is stowed away in common folks ready to show when the right time comes."

"Tell us one of them, and I'll bless you for a hint. No one knows the anguish of an author's spirit when he can't ring down the curtain on an effective tableau," said Randal, with a glance at his friends to ask their aid in eliciting an anecdote or reminiscence.

"Tell about the splendid fellow who held the bridge, like Horatius, till help came up. That was a thrilling story, I assure you," answered Sophie, with an inviting smile.

But Saul would not be his own hero, and said briefly:

"Any man can be brave when the battle-fever is on him, and it only takes a little physical courage to dash ahead." He paused a moment, with his eyes on the snowy landscape without, where twilight was deepening; then, as if constrained by the memory that winter scene evoked, he slowly continued,—

"One of the bravest things I ever knew was done by a poor fellow who has been a hero to me ever since, though I only met him that night. It was after one of the big battles of that last winter, and I was knocked over with a broken leg and two or three bullets here and there. Night was coming on, snow falling, and a sharp wind blew over the field where a lot of us lay, dead and alive, waiting for the ambulance to come and pick us up. There was skirmishing going on not far off, and our prospects were rather poor between frost and fire. I was calculating how I'd manage, when I found two poor chaps close by who were worse off, so I braced up and did what I could for them. One had an arm blown away, and kept up a dreadful groaning. The other was shot bad, and bleeding to death for want of help, but never complained. He was nearest, and I liked his pluck, for he spoke cheerful and made me ashamed to growl. Such times make dreadful brutes of men if they haven't something to hold on to, and all three of us were most wild with pain and cold and hunger, for we'd fought all day fasting, when we heard a rumble in the road below, and saw lanterns bobbing round. That meant life to us, and we all tried to holler; two of us, were pretty faint, but I managed a good yell, and they heard it.

"'Room for one more. Hard luck, old boys, but we are full and must save the worst wounded first. Take a drink, and hold on till we come back,' says one of them with the stretcher.

"'Here's the one to go,' I says, pointin' out my man, for I saw by the light that he was hard hit.

"'No, that one. He's got more chances than I, or this one; he's young and got a mother; I'll wait,' said the good feller, touchin' my arm, for he'd heard me mutterin' to myself about this dear old lady. We always want mother when we are down, you know."

Saul's eyes turned to the beloved face with a glance of tenderest affection, and Aunt Plumy answered with a dismal groan at the recollection of his need that night, and her absence.

"Well, to be short, the groaning chap was taken, and my man left. I was mad, but there was no time for talk, and the selfish one went off and left that poor feller to run his one chance. I had my rifle, and guessed I could hobble up to use it if need be; so we settled back to wait without much hope of help, everything being in a muddle. And wait we did till morning, for that ambulance did not come back till next day, when most of us were past needing it.

"I'll never forget that night. I dream it all over again as plain as if it was real. Snow, cold, darkness, hunger, thirst, pain, and all round us cries and cursing growing less and less, till at last only the wind went moaning over that meadow. It was awful! so lonesome, help- less, and seemingly God-forsaken. Hour after hour we lay there side by side under one coat, waiting to be saved or die, for the wind grew strong and we grew weak."

Saul drew a long breath, and held his hands to the fire as if he felt again the sharp suffering of that night.

"And the man?" asked Emily, softly, as if reluctant to break the silence.

"He *was* a man! In times like that men talk like brothers and show what they are. Lying there, slowly freezing, Joe Cummings told me about his wife and babies, his old folks waiting for him, all depending on him, yet all ready to give him up when he was needed. A plain man, but honest and true, and loving as a woman; I soon saw that as he went on talking, half to me and half to himself, for sometimes he wandered a little toward the end. I've read books, heard sermons, and seen good folks, but nothing ever came so close or did me so much good as seeing this man die. He had one chance and gave it cheerfully. He longed for those he loved, and let 'em go with a good-by they couldn't hear. He suffered all the pains we most shrink from without a murmur, and kept my heart warm while his own was growing cold. It's no use trying to tell that part of it; but I heard prayers that night that meant something, and I saw how faith could hold a soul up when everything was gone but God."

Saul stopped there with a sudden huskiness in his deep voice, and when he went on it was in the tone of one who speaks of a dear friend.

"Joe grew still by and by, and I thought he was asleep, for I felt his breath when I tucked him up, and his hand held on to mine. The cold sort of numbed me, and I dropped off, too weak and stupid to think or feel. I never should have waked up if it hadn't been for Joe. When I came to, it was morning, and I thought I was dead, for all I could see was that great field of white mounds, like graves, and a splendid sky above. Then I looked for Joe, remembering; but he had put my coat back over me, and lay stiff and still under the snow that covered him like a shroud, all except his face. A bit of my cape had blown over it, and when I took it off and the sun shone on his dead face, I declare to you it was so full of heavenly peace I felt as if that common man had been glorified by God's light, and rewarded by God's 'Well done.' That's all."

No one spoke for a moment, while the women wiped their eyes, and Saul dropped his as if to hide something softer than tears.

"It was very noble, very touching. And you? how did you get off at last?" asked Randal, with real admiration and respect in his usually languid face.

"Crawled off," answered Saul, relapsing into his former brevity of speech.

"Why not before, and save yourself all that misery?"

"Couldn't leave Joe."

"Ah, I see; there were two heroes that night."

"Dozens, I've no doubt. Those were times that made heroes of men, and women, too."

"Tell us more;" begged Emily, looking up with an expression none of her admirers ever brought to her face by their softest compliments or wiliest gossip.

"I've done my part. It's Mr. Randal's turn now;" and Saul drew himself out of the ruddy circle of firelight, as if ashamed of the prominent part he was playing.

Sophie and her friend had often heard Randal talk, for he was an accomplished *raconteur*, but that night he exerted himself, and was unusually brilliant and entertaining, as if upon his mettle. The Bassets were charmed. They sat late and were very merry, for Aunt Plumy got up a little supper for them, and her cider was as exhilarating as champagne. When they parted for the night and Sophie kissed her aunt, Emily did the same, saying heartily,—

"It seems as if I'd known you all my life, and this is certainly the most enchanting old place that ever was."

"Glad you like it, dear. But it ain't all fun, as you'll find out to-morrow when you go to work, for Sophie says you must," answered Mrs. Basset, as her guests trooped away, rashly promising to like everything.

They found it difficult to keep their word when they were called at half past six next morning. Their rooms were warm, however, and they managed to scramble down in time for breakfast, guided by the fragrance of coffee and Aunt Plumy's shrill voice singing the good old hymn—

> "Lord, in the morning Thou shalt hear
> My voice ascending high."

An open fire blazed on the hearth, for the cooking was done in the lean-to, and the spacious, sunny kitchen was kept in all its old-fashioned perfection, with the wooden settle in a warm nook, the tall clock behind the door, copper and pewter utensils shining on the dresser, old china in the corner closet and a little spinning wheel rescued from the garret by Sophie to adorn the deep window, full of scarlet geraniums, Christmas roses, and white chrysanthemums.

The young lady, in a checked apron and mob-cap, greeted her friends with a dish of buckwheats in one hand, and a pair of cheeks that proved she had been learning to fry these delectable cakes.

"You do 'keep it up' in earnest, upon my word; and very becoming it is, dear. But won't you ruin your complexion and roughen your hands if you do so much of this new fancy-work?" asked Emily, much amazed at this novel freak.

"I like it, and really believe I've found my proper sphere at last. Domestic life seems so pleasant to me that I feel as if I'd better keep it up for the rest of my life," answered Sophie, making a pretty picture of herself as she cut great slices of brown bread, with the early sunshine touching her happy face.

"The charming Miss Vaughan in the rôle of a farmer's wife. I find it difficult to imagine, and shrink from the thought of the wide-spread dismay such a fate will produce among her adorers," added Randal, as he basked in the glow of the hospitable fire.

"She might do worse; but come to breakfast and do honor to my handiwork," said Sophie, thinking of her worn-out millionaire, and rather nettled by the satiric smile on Randal's lips.

"What an appetite early rising gives one. I feel equal to almost anything, so let me help wash cups," said Emily, with unusual energy, when the hearty meal was over and Sophie began to pick up the dishes as if it was her usual work.

Ruth went to the window to water the flowers, and Randal followed to make himself agreeable, remembering her defence of him last night. He was used to admiration from feminine eyes, and flattery from soft lips, but found something new and charming in the innocent delight which showed itself at his approach in blushes more eloquent than words, and shy glances from eyes full of hero-worship.

"I hope you are going to spare me a posy for to-morrow night, since I can be fine in no other way to do honor to the dance Miss Sophie proposes for us," he said, leaning in the bay window to look down on the little girl, with the devoted air he usually wore for pretty women.

"Anything you like! I should be so glad to have you wear my flowers. There will be enough for all, and I've nothing else to give to people who have made me as happy as cousin Sophie and you," answered Ruth, half drowning her great calla as she spoke with grateful warmth.

"You must make her happy by accepting the invitation to go home with her which I heard given last night. A peep at the world would do you good, and be a pleasant change, I think."

"Oh, very pleasant! but would it do me good?" and Ruth looked up with sudden seriousness in her blue eyes, as a child questions an elder, eager, yet wistful.

"Why not?" asked Randal, wondering at the hesitation.

"I might grow discontented with things here if I saw splendid houses and fine people. I am very happy now, and it would break my heart to lose that happiness, or ever learn to be ashamed of home."

"But don't you long for more pleasure, new scenes and other friends than these?" asked the man, touched by the little creature's loyalty to the things she knew and loved.

"Very often, but mother says when I'm ready they will come, so I wait and try not to be impatient." But Ruth's eyes looked out over the green leaves as if the longing was very strong within her to see more of the unknown world lying beyond the mountains that hemmed her in.

"It is natural for birds to hop out of the nest, so I shall expect to see you over there before long, and ask you how you enjoy your first flight," said Randal, in a paternal tone that had a curious effect on Ruth.

To his surprise, she laughed, then blushed like one of her own roses, and answered with a demure dignity that was very pretty to see.

"I intend to hop soon, but it won't be a very long flight or very far from mother. She can't spare me, and nobody in the world can fill her place to me."

"Bless the child, does she think I'm going to make love to her," thought Randal, much amused, but quite mistaken. Wiser women had thought so when he assumed the caressing air with which he beguiled them into the little revelations of character he liked to use, as the south wind makes flowers open their hearts to give up their odor, then leaves them to carry it elsewhere, the more welcome for the stolen sweetness.

"Perhaps you are right. The maternal wing is a safe shelter for confiding little souls like you, Miss Ruth. You will be as comfortable here as your flowers in this sunny window," he said, carelessly pinching geranium leaves, and ruffling the roses till the pink petals of the largest fluttered to the floor.

As if she instinctively felt and resented something in the man which his act symbolized, the girl answered quietly, as she went on with her work, "Yes, if the frost does not touch me, or careless people spoil me too soon."

Before Randal could reply Aunt Plumy approached like a maternal hen who sees her chicken in danger.

"Saul is goin' to haul wood after he's done his chores, mebbe you'd like to go along? The view is good, the roads well broke, and the day uncommon fine."

"Thanks; it will be delightful, I dare say," politely responded the lion, with a secret shudder at the idea of a rural promenade at 8 A.M. in the winter.

"Come on, then; we'll feed the stock, and then I'll show you how to yoke oxen," said Saul, with a twinkle in his eye as he led the way, when his new aide had muffled himself up as if for a polar voyage.

"Now, that's too bad of Saul! He did it on purpose, just to please you, Sophie," cried Ruth presently, and the girls ran to the window to behold Randal bravely following his host with a pail of pigs' food in each hand, and an expression of resigned disgust upon his aristocratic face.

"To what base uses may we come," quoted Emily, as they all nodded and smiled upon the victim as he looked back from the barn-yard, where he was clamorously welcomed by his new charges.

"It is rather a shock at first, but it will do him good, and Saul won't be too hard upon him, I'm sure," said Sophie, going back to her work, while Ruth turned her best buds to the sun that they might be ready for a peace-offering to-morrow.

There was a merry clatter in the big kitchen for an hour; then Aunt Plumy and her daughter shut themselves up in the pantry to perform some culinary rites, and the young ladies went to inspect certain antique costumes laid forth in Sophie's room.

"You see, Em, I thought it would be appropriate to the house and season to have an old-fashioned dance. Aunt has quantities of ancient finery stowed away, for great-grandfather Basset was a fine old gentleman and his family lived in state. Take your choice of the crimson, blue or silver-gray damask. Ruth is to wear the worked muslin and quilted white satin skirt, with that coquettish hat."

"Being dark, I'll take the red and trim it up with this fine lace. You must wear the blue and primrose, with the distracting high-heeled shoes. Have you any suits for the men?" asked Emily, throwing herself at once into the all-absorbing matter of costume.

"A claret velvet coat and vest, silk stockings, cocked hat and snuff-box for Randal. Nothing large enough for Saul, so he must wear his uniform. Won't Aunt Plumy be superb in this plum-colored satin and immense cap?"

A delightful morning was spent in adapting the faded finery of the past to the blooming beauty of the present, and time and tongues flew till the toot of a horn called them down to dinner.

The girls were amazed to see Randal come whistling up the road with his trousers tucked into his boots, blue mittens on his hands, and an unusual amount of energy in his whole figure, as he drove the oxen, while Saul laughed at his vain attempts to guide the bewildered beasts.

"It's immense! The view from the hill is well worth seeing, for the snow glorifies the landscape and reminds one of Switzerland. I'm going to make a sketch of it this afternoon; better come and enjoy the delicious freshness, young ladies."

Randal was eating with such an appetite that he did not see the glances the girls exchanged as they promised to go.

"Bring home some more winter-green, I want things to be real nice, and we haven't enough for the kitchen," said Ruth, dimpling with girlish delight as she imagined herself dancing under the green garlands in her grandmother's wedding gown.

It was very lovely on the hill, for far as the eye could reach lay the wintry landscape sparkling with the brief beauty of sunshine on virgin snow. Pines sighed overhead, hardy birds flitted to and fro, and in all the trodden spots rose the little spires of evergreen ready for its Christmas duty. Deeper in the wood sounded the measured ring of axes, the crash of falling trees, while the red shirts of the men added color to the scene, and a fresh wind brought the aromatic breath of newly cloven hemlock and pine.

"How beautiful it is! I never knew before what winter woods were like. Did you, Sophie?" asked Emily, sitting on a stump to enjoy the novel pleasure at her ease.

"I've found out lately; Saul lets me come as often as I like, and this fine air seems to make a new creature of me," answered Sophie, looking about her with sparkling eyes, as if this was a kingdom where she reigned supreme.

"Something is making a new creature of you, that is very evident. I haven't yet discovered whether it is the air or some magic herb among that green stuff you are gathering so diligently;" and Emily laughed to see the color deepen beautifully in her friend's half-averted face.

"Scarlet is the only wear just now, I find. If we are lost like babes in the woods there are plenty of Red-breasts to cover us with leaves," and Randal joined Emily's laugh, with a glance at Saul, who had just pulled his coat off.

"You wanted to see this tree go down, so stand from under and I'll show you how it's done," said the farmer, taking up his axe, not unwilling to gratify his guests and display his manly accomplishments at the same time.

It was a fine sight, the stalwart man swinging his axe with magnificent strength and skill, each blow sending a thrill through the stately tree, till its heart was reached and it tottered to its fall. Never pausing for breath Saul shook his yellow mane out of his eyes, and hewed away, while the drops stood on his forehead and his arm ached, as bent on distinguishing himself as if he had been a knight tilting against his rival for his lady's favor.

"I don't know which to admire most, the man or his muscle. One doesn't often see such vigor, size and comeliness in these degenerate days," said Randal, mentally booking the fine figure in the red shirt.

"I think we have discovered a rough diamond. I only wonder if

Sophie is going to try and polish it," answered Emily, glancing at her friend, who stood a little apart, watching the rise and fall of the axe as intently as if her fate depended on it.

Down rushed the tree at last, and, leaving them to examine a crow's nest in its branches, Saul went off to his men, as if he found the praises of his prowess rather too much for him.

Randal fell to sketching, the girls to their garland-making, and for a little while the sunny woodland nook was full of lively chat and pleasant laughter, for the air exhilarated them all like wine. Suddenly a man came running from the wood, pale and anxious, saying, as he hastened by for help, "Blasted tree fell on him! Bleed to death before the doctor comes!"

"Who? who?" cried the startled trio.

But the man ran on, with some breathless reply, in which only a name was audible—"Basset."

"The deuce it is!" and Randal dropped his pencil, while the girls sprang up in dismay. Then, with one impulse, they hastened to the distant group, half visible behind the fallen trees and corded wood.

Sophie was there first, and forcing her way through the little crowd of men, saw a red-shirted figure on the ground, crushed and bleeding, and threw herself down beside it with a cry that pierced the hearts of those who heard it. In the act she saw it was not Saul, and covered her bewildered face as if to hide its joy. A strong arm lifted her, and the familiar voice said cheeringly,—

"I'm all right, dear. Poor Bruce is hurt, but we've sent for help. Better go right home and forget all about it."

"Yes, I will, if I can do nothing;" and Sophie meekly returned to her friends who stood outside the circle over which Saul's head towered, assuring them of his safety.

Hoping they had not seen her agitation, she led Emily away, leaving Randal to give what aid he could and bring them news of the poor wood-chopper's state.

Aunt Plumy produced the "camphire" the moment she saw Sophie's pale face, and made her lie down, while the brave old lady trudged briskly off with bandages and brandy to the scene of action. On her return she brought comfortable news of the man, so the little flurry blew over and was forgotten by all but Sophie, who remained pale and quiet all the evening, tying evergreen as if her life depended on it.

"A good night's sleep will set her up. She ain't used to such things, dear child, and needs cossetin'," said Aunt Plumy, purring over her until she was in her bed, with a hot stone at her feet and a bowl of herb tea to quiet her nerves.

An hour later, when Emily went up, she peeped in to see if Sophie was sleeping nicely, and was surprised to find the invalid wrapped in a dressing-gown writing busily.

"Last will and testament, or sudden inspiration, dear? How are you? faint or feverish, delirious or in the dumps! Saul looks so anxious, and Mrs. Basset hushes us all up so, I came to bed, leaving Randal to entertain Ruth."

As she spoke Emily saw the papers disappear in a portfolio, and Sophie rose with a yawn.

"I was writing letters, but I'm sleepy now. Quite over my foolish fright, thank you. Go and get your beauty sleep that you may dazzle the natives to-morrow."

"So glad, good night;" and Emily went away, saying to herself, "Something is going on, and I must find out what it is before I leave. Sophie can't blind *me*."

But Sophie did all the next day, being delightfully gay at the dinner, and devoting herself to the young minister who was invited to meet the distinguished novelist, and evidently being afraid of him, gladly basked in the smiles of his charming neighbor. A dashing sleigh-ride occupied the afternoon, and then great was the fun and excitement over the costumes.

Aunt Plumy laughed till the tears rolled down her cheeks as the girls compressed her into the plum-colored gown with its short waist, leg-of-mutton sleeves, and narrow skirt. But a worked scarf hid all deficiencies, and the towering cap struck awe into the soul of the most frivolous observer.

"Keep an eye on me, girls, for I shall certainly split somewheres or lose my head-piece off when I'm trottin' round. What would my blessed mother say if she could see me rigged out in her best things?" and with a smile and a sigh the old lady departed to look after "the boys," and see that the supper was all right.

Three prettier damsels never tripped down the wide staircase than the brilliant brunette in crimson brocade, the pensive blonde in blue, or the rosy little bride in old muslin and white satin.

A gallant court gentleman met them in the hall with a superb bow, and escorted them to the parlor, where Grandma Basset's ghost was discovered dancing with a modern major in full uniform.

Mutual admiration and many compliments followed, till other ancient ladies and gentlemen arrived in all manner of queer costumes, and the old house seemed to wake from its humdrum quietude to sudden music and merriment, as if a past generation had returned to keep its Christmas there.

The village fiddler soon struck up the good old tunes, and then the strangers saw dancing that filled them with mingled mirth and envy; it was so droll, yet so hearty. The young men, unusually awkward in their grandfathers' knee-breeches, flapping vests, and swallow-tail coats, footed it bravely with the buxom girls who were the prettier for their quaintness, and danced with such vigor that their high combs stood awry, their furbelows waved wildly, and their cheeks were as red as their breast-knots, or hose.

It was impossible to stand still, and one after the other the city folk yielded to the spell, Randal leading off with Ruth, Sophie swept away by Saul, and Emily being taken possession of by a young giant of eighteen, who spun her around with a boyish impetuosity that took her breath away. Even Aunt Plumy was discovered jigging it alone in the pantry, as if the music was too much for her, and the plates and glasses jingled gaily on the shelves in time to Money Musk and Fishers' Hornpipe.

A pause came at last, however, and fans fluttered, heated brows were wiped, jokes were made, lovers exchanged confidences, and every nook and corner held a man and maid carrying on the sweet game which is never out of fashion. There was a glitter of gold lace in the back entry, and a train of blue and primrose shone in the dim light. There was a richer crimson than that of the geraniums in the deep window, and a dainty shoe tapped the bare floor impatiently as the brilliant black eyes looked everywhere for the court gentleman, while their owner listened to the gruff prattle of an enamored boy. But in the upper hall walked a little white ghost as if waiting for some shadowy companion, and when a dark form appeared ran to take its arm, saying, in a tone of soft satisfaction,—

"I was so afraid you wouldn't come!"

"Why did you leave me, Ruth?" answered a manly voice in a tone of surprise, though the small hand slipping from the velvet coat-sleeve was replaced as if it was pleasant to feel it there.

A pause, and then the other voice answered demurely,—

"Because I was afraid my head would be turned by the fine things you were saying."

"It is impossible to help saying what one feels to such an artless little creature as you are. It does me good to admire anything so fresh and sweet, and won't harm you."

"It might if—"

"If what, my daisy?"

"I believed it," and a laugh seemed to finish the broken sentence better than the words.

"You may, Ruth, for I do sincerely admire the most genuine girl I have seen for a long time. And walking here with you in your bridal white I was just asking myself if I should not be a happier man with a home of my own and a little wife hanging on my arm than drifting about the world as I do now with only myself to care for."

"I know you would!" and Ruth spoke so earnestly that Randal was both touched and startled, fearing he had ventured too far in a mood of unwonted sentiment, born of the romance of the hour and the sweet frankness of his companion.

"Then you don't think it would be rash for some sweet woman to take me in hand and make me happy, since fame is a failure?"

"Oh, no; it would be easy work if she loved you. I know some one—if I only dared to tell her name."

"Upon my soul, this is cool," and Randal looked down, wondering if the audacious lady on his arm could be shy Ruth.

If he had seen the malicious merriment in her eyes he would have been more humiliated still, but they were modestly averted, and the face under the little hat was full of a soft agitation rather dangerous even to a man of the world.

"She is a captivating little creature, but it is too soon for anything but a mild flirtation. I must delay further innocent revelations or I shall do something rash."

While making this excellent resolution Randal had been pressing the hand upon his arm and gently pacing down the dimly lighted hall with the sound of music in his ears, Ruth's sweetest roses in his button-hole, and a loving little girl beside him, as he thought.

"You shall tell me by and by when we are in town. I am sure you will come, and meanwhile don't forget me."

"I am going in the spring, but I shall not be with Sophie," answered Ruth, in a whisper.

"With whom then? I shall long to see you."

"With my husband. I am to be married in May."

"The deuce you are!" escaped Randal, as he stopped short to stare at his companion, sure she was not in earnest.

But she was, for as he looked the sound of steps coming up the back stairs made her whole face flush and brighten with the unmistakable glow of happy love, and she completed Randal's astonishment by running into the arms of the young minister, saying with an irrepressible laugh, "Oh! John, why didn't you come before?"

The court gentleman was all right in a moment, and the coolest of the three as he offered his congratulations and gracefully retired, leaving the lovers to enjoy the tryst he had delayed. But as he went down stairs his brows were knit, and he slapped the broad railing smartly with his cocked hat as if some irritation must find vent in a more energetic way than merely saying, "Confound the little baggage!" under his breath.

Such an amazing supper came from Aunt Plumy's big pantry that the city guests could not eat for laughing at the queer dishes circulating through the rooms, and copiously partaken of by the hearty young folks.

Doughnuts and cheese, pie and pickles, cider and tea, baked beans and custards, cake and cold turkey, bread and butter, plum pudding and French bonbons, Sophie's contribution.

"May I offer you the native delicacies, and share your plate. Both are very good, but the china has run short, and after such vigorous exercise as you have had you must need refreshment. I'm sure I do!" said Randal, bowing before Emily with a great blue platter laden with two doughnuts, two wedges of pumpkin pie and two spoons.

The smile with which she welcomed him, the alacrity with which she made room beside her and seemed to enjoy the supper he brought, was so soothing to his ruffled spirit that he soon began to feel that there is no friend like an old friend, that it would not be difficult to name a sweet woman who would take him in hand and would make him happy if he cared to ask her, and he began to think he would by and by, it was so pleasant to sit in that green corner with waves of crimson brocade flowing over his feet, and a fine face softening beautifully under his eyes.

The supper was not romantic, but the situation was, and Emily found that pie ambrosial food eaten with the man she loved, whose eyes talked more eloquently than the tongue just then busy with a doughnut. Ruth kept away, but glanced at them as she served her company, and her own happy experience helped her to see that all was going well in that quarter. Saul and Sophie emerged from the back entry with shining countenances, but carefully avoided each other for the rest of the evening. No one observed this but Aunt Plumy from the recesses of her pantry, and she folded her hands as if well content, as she murmured fervently over a pan full of crullers, "Bless the dears! Now I can die happy."

Every one thought Sophie's old-fashioned dress immensely becoming, and several of his former men said to Saul with blunt admiration, "Major, you look to-night as you used to after we'd gained a big battle."

"I feel as if I had," answered the splendid Major, with eyes much brighter than his buttons, and a heart under them infinitely prouder than when he was promoted on the field of honor, for his Waterloo was won.

There was more dancing, followed by games, in which Aunt Plumy shone pre-eminent, for the supper was off her mind and she could enjoy herself. There were shouts of merriment as the blithe old lady twirled the platter, hunted the squirrel, and went to Jerusalem like a girl of sixteen; her cap in a ruinous condition, and every seam of the purple dress straining like sails in a gale. It was great fun, but at midnight it came to an end, and the young folks, still bubbling over with innocent jollity, went jingling away along the snowy hills, unanimously pronouncing Mrs. Basset's party the best of the season.

"Never had such a good time in my life!" exclaimed Sophie, as the family stood together in the kitchen where the candles among the wreaths were going out, and the floor was strewn with wrecks of past joy.

"I'm proper glad, dear. Now you all go to bed and lay as late as you like to-morrow. I'm so kinder worked up I couldn't sleep, so Saul and me will put things to rights without a mite of noise to disturb you;" and Aunt Plumy sent them off with a smile that was a benediction, Sophie thought.

"The dear old soul speaks as if midnight was an unheard-of hour for Christians to be up. What would she say if she knew how we seldom go to bed till dawn in the ball season? I'm so wide awake I've half a mind to pack a little. Randal must go at two, he says, and we shall want his escort," said Emily, as the girls laid away their brocades in the great press in Sophie's room.

"I'm not going. Aunt can't spare me, and there is nothing to go for yet," answered Sophie, beginning to take the white chrysanthemums out of her pretty hair.

"My dear child, you will die of ennui up here. Very nice for a week or so, but frightful for a winter. We are going to be very gay, and cannot get on without you," cried Emily, dismayed at the suggestion.

"You will have to, for I'm not coming. I am very happy here, and so tired of the frivolous life I lead in town, that I have decided to try a better one," and Sophie's mirror reflected a face full of the sweetest content.

"Have you lost your mind? experienced religion? or any other dreadful thing? You always were odd, but this last freak is the strangest of all. What will your guardian say, and the world?" added Emily in the awe-stricken tone of one who stood in fear of the omnipotent Mrs. Grundy.

"Guardy will be glad to be rid of me, and I don't care that for the world," cried Sophie, snapping her fingers with a joyful sort of recklessness which completed Emily's bewilderment.

"But Mr. Hammond? Are you going to throw away millions, lose your chance of making the best match in the city, and driving the girls of our set out of their wits with envy?"

Sophie laughed at her friend's despairing cry, and turning round said quietly,—

"I wrote to Mr. Hammond last night, and this evening received my reward for being an honest girl. Saul and I are to be married in the spring when Ruth is."

Emily fell prone upon the bed as if the announcement was too much for her, but was up again in an instant to declare with prophetic solemnity,—

"I knew something was going on, but hoped to get you away before you were lost. Sophie, you will repent. Be warned, and forget this sad delusion."

"Too late for that. The pang I suffered yesterday when I thought Saul was dead showed me how well I loved him. To-night he asked me to stay, and no power in the world can part us. Oh! Emily, it is all so sweet, so beautiful, that *everything* is possible, and I know I shall be happy in this dear old home, full of love and peace and honest hearts. I only hope you may find as true and tender a man to live for as my Saul."

Sophie's face was more eloquent than her fervent words, and Emily beautifully illustrated the inconsistency of her sex by suddenly embracing her friend, with the incoherent exclamation, "I think I have, dear! Your brave Saul is worth a dozen old Hammonds, and I do believe you are right."

It is unnecessary to tell how, as if drawn by the irresistible magic of sympathy, Ruth and her mother crept in one by one to join the midnight conference and add their smiles and tears, tender hopes and proud delight to the joys of that memorable hour. Nor how Saul, unable to sleep, mounted guard below, and meeting Randal prowling down to soothe his nerves with a surreptitious cigar found it impossible to help confiding to his attentive ear the happiness that would break bounds and overflow in unusual eloquence.

Peace fell upon the old house at last, and all slept as if some magic herb had touched their eyelids, bringing blissful dreams and a glad awakening.

"Can't we persuade you to come with us, Miss Sophie?" asked Randal next day, as they made their adieux.

"I'm under orders now, and dare not disobey my superior officer," answered Sophie, handing her Major his driving gloves, with a look which plainly showed that she had joined the great army of devoted women who enlist for life and ask no pay but love.

"I shall depend on being invited to your wedding, then, and

yours, too, Miss Ruth," added Randal, shaking hands with "the little baggage," as if he had quite forgiven her mockery and forgotten his own brief lapse into sentiment.

Before she could reply Aunt Plumy said, in a tone of calm conviction, that made them all laugh, and some of them look conscious,—

"Spring is a good time for weddin's, and I shouldn't wonder if there was quite a number."

"Nor I;" and Saul and Sophie smiled at one another as they saw how carefully Randal arranged Emily's wraps.

Then with kisses, thanks and all the good wishes that happy hearts could imagine, the guests drove away, to remember long and gratefully that pleasant country Christmas.

WHAT THE BELLS SAW AND SAID
FROM PROVERB TALES

"Bells ring others to church, but go not in themselves."

NO one saw the spirits of the bells up there in the old steeple at midnight on Christmas Eve. Six quaint figures, each wrapped in a shadowy cloak and wearing a bell-shaped cap. All were gray-headed, for they were among the oldest bell-spirits of the city, and "the light of other days" shone in their thoughtful eyes. Silently they sat, looking down on the snow-covered roofs glittering in the moonlight, and the quiet streets deserted by all but the watchmen on their chilly rounds, and such poor souls as wandered shelterless in the winter night. Presently one of the spirits said, in a tone, which, low as it was, filled the belfry with reverberating echoes,—

"Well, brothers, are your reports ready of the year that now lies dying?"

All bowed their heads, and one of the oldest answered in a sonorous voice:—

"My report isn't all I could wish. You know I look down on the commercial part of our city and have fine opportunities for seeing what goes on there. It's my business to watch the business men, and upon my word I'm heartily ashamed of them sometimes. During the war they did nobly, giving their time and money, their sons and selves to the good cause, and I was proud of them. But now too many of them have fallen back into the old ways, and their motto seems to be, 'Every one for himself, and the devil take the hindmost.' Cheating, lying and stealing are hard words, and I don't mean to apply them to *all* who swarm about below there like ants on an ant-hill—*they* have other names for these things, but I'm old-fashioned and use plain words. There's a deal too much dishonesty in the world, and business seems to have become a game of hazard in which luck, not labor, wins the prize. When I was young, men were years making moderate fortunes, and were satisfied with them. They built them on sure foundations, knew how to enjoy them while they lived, and to leave a good name behind them when they died.

"Now it's anything for money; health, happiness, honor, life itself, are flung down on that great gaming-table, and they forget everything else in the excitement of success or the desperation of defeat. Nobody seems satisfied either, for those who win have little time or taste to enjoy their prosperity, and those who lose have little courage or patience to support them in adversity. They don't even fail as they used to. In my day when a merchant found himself embarrassed he didn't ruin others in order to save himself, but honestly confessed the truth, gave up everything, and began again. But now-a-days after all manner of dishonorable shifts there comes a grand crash; many suffer, but by some hocus-pocus the merchant saves enough to retire upon and live comfortably here or abroad. It's very evident that honor and honesty don't mean now what they used to mean in the days of old May, Higginson and Lawrence.

"They preach below here, and very well too sometimes, for I often slide down the rope to peep and listen during service. But, bless you! they don't seem to lay either sermon, psalm or prayer to heart, for while the minister is doing his best, the congregation, tired with the breathless hurry of the week, sleep peacefully, calculate their chances for the morrow, or wonder which of their neighbors will lose or win in the great game. Don't tell me! I've seen them do it, and if I dared I'd have startled every soul of them with a rousing peal. Ah, they don't dream whose eye is on them, they never guess what secrets the telegraph wires tell as the messages fly by, and little know what a report I give to the winds of heaven as I ring out above them morning, noon, and night." And the old spirit shook his head till the tassel on his cap jangled like a little bell.

"There are some, however, whom I love and honor," he said, in a benignant tone, "who honestly earn their bread, who deserve all the success that comes to them, and always keep a warm corner in their noble hearts for those less blest than they. These are the men who serve the city in times of peace, save it in times of war, deserve the highest honors in its gift, and leave behind them a record that keeps their memories green. For such an one we lately tolled a knell, my brothers; and as our united voices pealed over the city, in all grateful hearts, sweeter and more solemn than any chime, rung the words that made him so beloved,—

"'Treat our dead boys tenderly, and send them home to me.'"

He ceased, and all the spirits reverently uncovered their gray heads as a strain of music floated up from the sleeping city and died among the stars.

"Like yours, my report is not satisfactory in all respects," began the second spirit, who wore a very pointed cap and a finely-ornamented cloak. But, though his dress was fresh and youthful, his face was old, and he had nodded several times during his brother's speech. "My greatest affliction during the past year has been the terrible extravagance which prevails. My post, as you know, is at the court end of the city, and I see all the fashionable vices and follies. It is a marvel to me how so many of these immortal creatures, with such opportunities for usefulness, self-improvement and genuine happiness can be content to go round and round in one narrow circle of unprofitable and unsatisfactory pursuits. I do my best to warn them; Sunday after Sunday I chime in their ears the beautiful old hymns that sweetly chide or cheer the hearts that truly listen and believe; Sunday after Sunday I look down on them as they pass in, hoping to see that my words have not fallen upon deaf ears; and Sunday after Sunday they listen to words that should teach them much, yet seem to go by them like the wind. They are told to love their neighbor, yet too many hate him because he possesses more of this world's goods or honors than they; they are told that a rich man cannot enter the kingdom of heaven, yet they go on laying up perishable wealth, and though often warned that moth and rust will corrupt, they fail to believe it till the worm that destroys enters and mars their own chapel of ease. Being a spirit, I see below external splendor and find much poverty of heart and soul under the velvet and the ermine which should cover rich and royal natures. Our city saints walk abroad in threadbare suits, and under quiet bonnets shine the eyes that make sunshine in the shady places. Often as I watch the glittering procession passing to and fro below me, I wonder if, with all our progress, there is to-day as much real piety as in the times when our fathers, poorly clad, with weapon in one hand and Bible in the other, came weary distances to worship in the wilderness with fervent faith unquenched by danger, suffering and solitude.

"Yet in spite of my fault-finding I love my children, as I call them, for all are not butterflies. Many find wealth no temptation to forgetfulness of duty or hardness of heart. Many give freely of their abundance, pity the poor, comfort the afflicted, and make our city loved and honored in other lands as in our own. They have their cares, losses, and heartaches as well as the poor; it isn't all sunshine with them, and they learn, poor souls, that

> *'Into each life some rain must fall,*
> *Some days must be dark and dreary.'*

"But I've hopes of them, and lately they have had a teacher so genial, so gifted, so well-beloved that all who listen to him must be better for the lessons of charity, good-will and cheerfulness which he brings home to them by the magic of tears and smiles. We know him, we love him, we always remember him as the year comes round, and the blithest song our brazen tongues utter is a Christmas carol to the Father of 'The Chimes!'"

As the spirit spoke his voice grew cheery, his old face shone, and in a burst of hearty enthusiasm he flung up his cap and cheered like a boy. So did the others, and as the fairy shout echoed through the belfry a troop of shadowy figures, with faces lovely or grotesque, tragical or gay, sailed by on the wings of the wintry wind and waved their hands to the spirits of the bells.

As the excitement subsided and the spirits reseated themselves, looking ten years younger for that burst, another spoke. A venerable brother in a dingy mantle, with a tuneful voice, and eyes that seemed to have grown sad with looking on much misery.

"He loves the poor, the man we've just hurrahed for, and he makes others love and remember them, bless him!" said the spirit. "I hope he'll touch the hearts of those who listen to him here and beguile them to open their hands to my unhappy children over yonder. If I could set some of the forlorn souls in my parish beside the happier creatures who weep over imaginary woes as they are painted by his eloquent lips, that brilliant scene would be better than any sermon. Day and night I look down on lives as full of sin, self-sacrifice and suffering as any in those famous books. Day and night I try to comfort the poor by my cheery voice, and to make their wants known by proclaiming them with all my might. But people seem to be so intent on business, pleasure or home duties that they have no time to hear and answer my appeal. There's a deal of charity in this good city, and when the people do wake up they work with a will; but I can't help thinking that if some of the money lavished on luxuries was spent on necessaries for the poor, there would be fewer tragedies like that which ended yesterday. It's a short story, easy to tell, though long and hard to live; listen to it.

"Down yonder in the garret of one of the squalid houses at the foot of my tower, a little girl has lived for a year, fighting silently and single-handed a good fight against poverty and sin. I saw her when she first came, a hopeful, cheerful, brave-hearted little soul, alone, yet not afraid. She used to sit all day sewing at her window, and her lamp burnt far into the night, for she was very poor, and all she earned would barely give her food and shelter. I watched her feed the doves, who seemed to be her only friends; she never forgot them, and daily gave them the few crumbs that fell from her meagre table. But there was no kind hand to feed and foster the little human dove, and so she starved.

"For a while she worked bravely, but the poor three dollars a week would not clothe and feed and warm her, though the things her busy fingers made sold for enough to keep her comfortably if she had received it. I saw the pretty color fade from her cheeks; her eyes grew hollow, her voice lost its cheery ring, her step its elasticity, and her face began to wear the haggard, anxious look that made its youth doubly pathetic. Her poor little gowns grew shabby, her shawl so thin she shivered when the pitiless wind smote her, and her feet were almost bare. Rain and snow beat on the patient little figure going to and fro, each morning with hope and courage faintly shining, each evening with the shadow of despair gathering darker round her. It was a hard time for all, desperately hard for her, and in her poverty, sin and pleasure tempted her. She resisted, but as another bitter winter came she feared that in her misery she might yield, for body and soul were weakened now by the long struggle. She knew not where to turn for help; there seemed to be no place for her at any safe and happy fireside; life's hard aspect daunted her, and she turned to death, saying confidingly, 'Take me while I'm innocent and not afraid to go.'

"I saw it all! I saw how she sold everything that would bring money and paid her little debts to the utmost penny; how she set her poor room in order for the last time; how she tenderly bade the doves good-by, and lay down on her bed to die. At nine o'clock last night as my bell rang over the city, I tried to tell what was going on in the garret where the light was dying out so fast. I cried to them with all my strength,—

"'Kind souls, below there! a fellow-creature is perishing for lack of charity! Oh, help her before it is too late! Mothers, with little daughters on your knees, stretch out your hands and take her in! Happy women, in the safe shelter of home, think of her desolation! Rich men, who grind the faces of the poor, remember that this soul will one day be required of you! Dear Lord, let not this little sparrow fall to the ground! Help, Christian men and women, in the name of Him whose birthday blessed the world!'

"Ah me! I rang, and clashed, and cried in vain. The passers-by only said, as they hurried home, laden with Christmas cheer: 'The old bell is merry to-night, as it should be at this blithe season, bless it!'

"As the clocks struck ten, the poor child lay down, saying, as she drank the last bitter draught life could give her, 'It's very cold, but soon I shall not feel it;' and with her quiet eyes fixed on the cross that glimmered in the moonlight above me, she lay waiting for the sleep that needs no lullaby.

"As the clock struck eleven, pain and poverty for her were over. It was bitter cold, but she no longer felt it. She lay serenely sleeping, with tired heart and hands, at rest forever. As the clocks struck twelve, the dear Lord remembered her, and with fatherly hand led her into the home where there is room for all. To-day I rung her knell, and though my heart was heavy, yet my soul was glad; for in spite of all her human woe and weakness, I am sure that little girl will keep a joyful Christmas up in heaven."

In the silence which the spirits for a moment kept, a breath of softer air than any from the snowy world below swept through the steeple and seemed to whisper, "Yes!"

"Avast there! fond as I am of salt water, I don't like this kind," cried the breezy voice of the fourth spirit, who had a tiny ship instead of a tassel on his cap, and who wiped his wet eyes with the sleeve of his rough blue cloak. "It won't take me long to spin my yarn; for things are pretty taut and ship-shape aboard our craft. Captain Taylor is an experienced sailor, and has brought many a ship safely into port in spite of wind and tide, and the devil's own whirlpools and hurricanes. If you want to see earnestness come aboard some Sunday when the Captain's on the quarter-deck, and take an observation. No danger of falling asleep there, no more than there is up aloft, 'when the stormy winds do blow.' Consciences get raked fore and aft, sins are blown clean out of the water, false colors are hauled down and true ones run up to the masthead, and many an immortal soul is warned to steer off in time from the pirates, rocks and quicksands of temptation. He's a regular revolving light, is the Captain,—a beacon always burning and saying plainly, 'Here are life-boats, ready to put off in all weathers and bring the shipwrecked into quiet waters.' He comes but seldom now, being laid up in the home dock, tranquilly waiting till his turn comes to go out with the tide and safely ride at anchor in the great harbor of the Lord. Our crew varies a good deal. Some of 'em have rather rough voyages, and come into port pretty well battered; land-sharks full foul of a good many, and do a deal of damage; but most of 'em carry brave and tender hearts under the blue jackets, for their rough nurse, the sea, manages to keep something of the child alive in the grayest old tar that makes the world his picture-book. We try to supply 'em with life-preservers while at sea, and make 'em feel sure of a hearty welcome when ashore, and I believe the year '67 will sail away into eternity with a satisfactory cargo. Brother North-End made me pipe my eye; so I'll make him laugh to pay for it, by telling a clerical joke I heard the other day. Bell-ows didn't make it, though he might have done so, as he's a connection of ours, and knows how to use his tongue as well as any of us. Speaking of the bells of a certain town, a reverend gentleman affirmed that each bell uttered an appropriate remark so plainly, that the words were audible to all. The Baptist bell cried, briskly, 'Come up and be dipped! come up and be dipped!' The Episcopal bell slowly said, 'Apos-tol-ic suc-cess-ion! apos-tol-ic suc-cess-ion!' The Orthodox bell solemnly pronounced, 'Eternal damnation! eternal damnation!' and the Methodist shouted, invitingly, 'Room for all! room for all!'"

As the spirit imitated the various calls, as only a jovial bell-sprite could, the others gave him a chime of laughter, and vowed they would each adopt some tune-ful summons, which should reach human ears and draw human feet more willingly to church.

"Faith, brother, you've kept your word and got the laugh out of us," cried a stout, sleek spirit, with a kindly face, and a row of little saints round his cap and a rosary at his side. "It's very well we are doing this year; the cathedral is full, the flock increasing, and the true faith holding its own entirely. Ye may shake your heads if you will and fear there'll be trouble, but I doubt it. We've warm hearts of our own, and the best of us don't forget that when we were starving, America—the saints bless the jewel!—sent us bread; when we were dying for lack of work, America opened her arms and took us in, and now helps us to build churches, homes and schools by giving us a share of the riches all men work for and win. It's a generous nation ye are, and a brave one, and we showed our gratitude by fighting for ye in the day of trouble and giving ye our Phil, and many another broth of a boy. The land is wide enough for us both, and while we work and fight and grow together, each may learn something from the other. I'm free to confess that your religion looks a bit cold and hard to me, even here in the good city where each man may ride his own hobby to death, and hoot at his neighbors as much as he will. You seem to keep your piety shut up all the week in your bare, white churches, and only let it out on Sundays, just a trifle musty with disuse. You set your rich, warm and soft to the fore, and leave the poor shivering at the door. You give your people bare walls to look upon, commonplace music to listen to, dull sermons to put them asleep, and then wonder why they stay away, or take no interest when they come.

"We leave our doors open day and night; our lamps are always burning, and we may come into our Father's house at any hour. We let rich and poor kneel together, all being equal there. With us abroad you'll see prince and peasant side by side, school-boy and bishop, market-woman and noble lady, saint and sinner, praying to the Holy Mary, whose motherly arms are open to high and low. We make our churches inviting with immortal music, pictures by the world's great masters, and rites that are splendid symbols of the faith we hold. Call it mummery if ye like, but let me ask you why so many of your sheep stray into our fold? It's because they miss the warmth, the hearty, the maternal tenderness which all souls love and long for, and fail to find in your stern, Puritanical belief. By Saint Peter! I've seen many a lukewarm worshipper, who for years has nodded in your cushioned pews, wake and glow with something akin to genuine piety while kneeling on the stone pavement of one of our cathedrals, with Raphael's angels before his eyes, with strains of magnificent music in his ears, and all about him, in shapes of power or beauty, the saints and martyrs who have saved the world, and whose presence inspires him to follow their divine example. It's not complaining of ye I am, but just reminding ye that men are but children after all, and need more tempting to virtue than they do to vice, which last comes easy to 'em since the Fall. Do your best in your own ways to get the poor souls into bliss, and good luck to ye. But remember, there's room in the Holy Mother Church for all, and when your own priests send ye to the divil, come straight to us and we'll take ye in."

"A truly Catholic welcome, bull and all," said the sixth spirit, who, in spite of his old-fashioned garments, had a youthful face, earnest, fearless eyes, and an energetic voice that woke the echoes with its vigorous tones. "I've a hopeful report, brothers, for the reforms of the day are wheeling into rank and marching on. The war isn't over nor rebeldom conquered yet, but the Old Guard has been 'up and at 'em' through the year. There has been some hard fighting, rivers of ink have flowed, and the Washington dawdlers have signalized themselves by a 'masterly inactivity.' The political campaign has been an anxious one; some of the leaders have deserted; some been mustered out; some have fallen gallantly, and as yet have received no monuments. But at the Grand Review the Cross of the Legion of Honor will surely shine on many a brave breast that won no decoration but its virtue here; for the world's fanatics make heaven's heroes, poets say.

"The flock of Nightingales that flew South during the 'winter of our discontent' are all at home again, some here and some in Heaven. But the music of their womanly heroism still lingers in the nation's memory, and makes a tender minor-chord in the battle-hymn of freedom.

"The reform in literature isn't as vigorous as I could wish; but a sharp attack of mental and moral dyspepsia will soon teach our people that French confectionery and the bad pastry of Wood, Braddon, Yates & Co. is not the best diet for the rising generation.

"Speaking of the rising generation reminds me of the schools. They are doing well; they always are, and we are justly proud of them. There may be a slight tendency toward placing too much value upon book-learning; too little upon home culture. Our girls are acknowledged to be uncommonly pretty, witty and wise, but some of us wish they had more health and less excitement, more domestic accomplishments and fewer ologies and isms, and were contented with simple pleasures and the old-fashioned virtues, and not quite so fond of the fast, frivolous life that makes them old so soon. I am fond of our girls and boys. I love to ring for their christenings and marriages, to toll proudly for the brave lads in blue, and tenderly for the innocent creatures whose seats are empty under my old roof. I want to see them anxious to make Young America a model of virtue, strength and beauty, and I believe they will in time.

"There have been some important revivals in religion; for the world won't stand still, and we must keep pace or be left behind to fossilize. A free nation must have a religion broad enough to embrace all mankind, deep enough to fathom and fill the human soul, high enough to reach the source of all love and wisdom, and pure enough to satisfy the wisest and the best. Alarm bells have been rung, anathemas pronounced, and Christians, forgetful of their creed, have abused one another heartily. But the truth always triumphs in the end, and whoever sincerely believes, works and waits for it, by whatever name he calls it, will surely find his own faith blessed to him in proportion to his charity for the faith of others.

"But look!—the first red streaks of dawn are in the East. Our vigil is over, and we must fly home to welcome in the holidays. Before we part, join with me, brothers, in resolving that through the coming year we will with all our hearts and tongues,—

> *'Ring out the old, ring in the new,*
> *Ring out the false, ring in the true;*
> *Ring in the valiant man and free,*
> *Ring in the Christ that is to be.'"*

Then hand in hand the spirits of the bells floated away, singing in the hush of dawn the sweet song the stars sung over Bethlehem, —"Peace on earth, good will to men."

A CHRISTMAS TURKEY, AND HOW IT CAME

"I know we couldn't do it."

"I say we could, if we all helped."

"How can we?"

"I've planned lots of ways; only you mustn't laugh at them, and you mustn't say a word to mother. I want it to be all a surprise."

"She 'll find us out."

"No, she won't, if we tell her we won't get into mischief."

"Fire away, then, and let's hear your fine plans."

"We must talk softly, or we shall wake father. He's got a headache."

A curious change came over the faces of the two boys as their sister lowered her voice, with a nod toward a half-opened door. They looked sad and ashamed, and Kitty sighed as she spoke, for all knew that father's headaches always began by his coming home stupid or cross, with only a part of his wages; and mother always cried when she thought they did not see her, and after the long sleep father looked as if he didn't like to meet their eyes, but went off early.

They knew what it meant, but never spoke of it,--only pondered over it, and mourned with mother at the change which was slowly altering their kind industrious father into a moody man, and mother into an anxious over-worked woman.

Kitty was thirteen, and a very capable girl, who helped with the housekeeping, took care of the two little ones, and went to school. Tommy and Sammy looked up to her and thought her a remarkably good sister. Now, as they sat round the stove having "a go-to-bed warm," the three heads were close together; and the boys listened eagerly to Kitty's plans, while the rattle of the sewing-machine in another room went on as tirelessly as it had done all day, for mother's work was more and more needed every month.

"Well!" began Kitty, in an impressive tone, "we all know that there won't be a bit of Christmas in this family if we don't make it. Mother's too busy, and father don't care, so we must see what we can do; for I should be mortified to death to go to school and say I hadn't had any turkey or plum-pudding. Don't expect presents; but we *must* have some kind of a decent dinner."

"So I say; I'm tired of fish and potatoes," said Sammy, the younger.

"But where's the dinner coming from?" asked Tommy, who had already taken some of the cares of life on his young shoulders, and knew that Christmas dinners did not walk into people's houses without money.

"We 'll earn it;" and Kitty looked like a small Napoleon planning the passage of the Alps. "You, Tom, must go early to-morrow to Mr. Brisket and offer to carry baskets. He will be dreadfully busy, and want you, I know; and you are so strong you can lug as much as some of the big fellows. He pays well, and if he won't give much money, you can take your wages in things to eat. We want everything."

"What shall I do?" cried Sammy, while Tom sat turning this plan over in his mind.

"Take the old shovel and clear sidewalks. The snow came on purpose to help you."

"It's awful hard work, and the shovel's half gone," began Sammy, who preferred to spend his holiday coasting on an old tea-tray.

"Don't growl, or you won't get any dinner," said Tom, making up his mind to lug baskets for the good of the family, like a manly lad as he was.

"I," continued Kitty, "have taken the hardest part of all; for after my work is done, and the babies safely settled, I 'm going to beg for the leavings of the holly and pine swept out of the church down below, and make some wreaths and sell them."

"If you can," put in Tommy, who had tried pencils, and failed to make a fortune.

"Not in the street?" cried Sam, looking alarmed.

"Yes, at the corner of the Park. I 'm bound to make some money, and don't see any other way. I shall put on an old hood and shawl, and no one will know me. Don't care if they do." And Kitty tried to mean what she said, but in her heart she felt that it would be a trial to her pride if any of her schoolmates should happen to recognize her.

"Don't believe you 'll do it."

"See if I don't; for I *will* have a good dinner one day in the year."

"Well, it doesn't seem right for us to do it. Father ought to take care of us, and we only buy some presents with the little bit we earn. He never gives us anything now." And Tommy scowled at the bedroom door, with a strong sense of injury struggling with affection in his boyish heart.

"Hush!" cried Kitty. "Don't blame him. Mother says we never must forget he's our father. I try not to; but when she cries, it's hard to feel as I ought." And a sob made the little girl stop short as she poked the fire to hide the trouble in the face that should have been all smiles.

For a moment the room was very still, as the snow beat on the window, and the fire-light flickered over the six shabby little boots put up on the stove hearth to dry.

Tommy's cheerful voice broke the silence, saying stoutly, "Well, if I 've got to work all day, I guess I 'll go to bed early. Don't fret, Kit. We 'll help all we can, and have a good time; see if we don't."

"I 'll go out real early, and shovel like fury. Maybe I 'll get a dollar. Would that buy a turkey?" asked Sammy, with the air of a millionaire.

"No, dear; one big enough for us would cost two, I 'm afraid. Perhaps we 'll have one sent us. We belong to the church, though folks don't know how poor we are now, and we can't beg." And Kitty bustled about, clearing up, rather exercised in her mind about going and asking for the much-desired fowl.

Soon all three were fast asleep, and nothing but the whir of the machine broke the quiet that fell upon the house. Then from the inner room a man came and sat over the fire with his head in his hands and his eyes fixed on the ragged little boots left to dry. He had heard the children's talk; and his heart was very heavy as he looked about the shabby room that used to be so neat and pleasant. What he thought no one knows, what he did we shall see by-and-by; but the sorrow and shame and tender silence of his children worked a miracle that night more lasting and lovely than the white beauty which the snow wrought upon the sleeping city.

Bright and early the boys were away to their work; while Kitty sang as she dressed the little sisters, put the house in order, and made her mother smile at the mysterious hints she gave of something splendid which was going to happen. Father was gone, and though all rather dreaded evening, nothing was said; but each worked with a will, feeling that Christmas should be merry in spite of poverty and care.

All day Tommy lugged fat turkeys, roasts of beef, and every sort of vegetable for other people's good dinners on the morrow, wondering meanwhile where his own was coming from. Mr. Brisket had an army of boys trudging here and there, and was too busy to notice any particular lad till the hurry was over, and only a few belated buyers remained to be served. It was late; but the stores kept open, and though so tired he could hardly stand, brave

Tommy held on when the other boys left, hoping to earn a trifle more by extra work. He sat down on a barrel to rest during a leisure moment, and presently his weary head nodded sideways into a basket of cranberries, where he slept quietly till the sound of gruff voices roused him.

It was Mr. Brisket scolding because one dinner had been forgotten.

"I told that rascal Beals to be sure and carry it, for the old gentleman will be in a rage if it doesn't come, and take away his custom. Every boy gone, and I can't leave the store, nor you either, Pat, with all the clearing up to do."

"Here's a by, sir, slapin illigant forninst the cranberries, bad luck to him!" answered Pat, with a shake that set poor Tom on his legs, wide awake at once.

"*Good* luck to him, you mean. Here, What's-your-name, you take this basket to that number, and I 'll make it worth your while," said Mr. Brisket, much relieved by this unexpected help.

"All right, sir;" and Tommy trudged off as briskly as his tired legs would let him, cheering the long cold walk with visions of the turkey with which his employer might reward him, for there were piles of them, and Pat was to have one for his family.

His brilliant dreams were disappointed, however, for Mr. Brisket naturally supposed Tom's father would attend to that part of the dinner, and generously heaped a basket with vegetables, rosy apples, and a quart of cranberries.

"There, if you ain't too tired, you can take one more load to that number, and a merry Christmas to you!" said the stout man, handing over his gift with the promised dollar.

"Thank you, sir; good-night," answered Tom, shouldering his last load with a grateful smile, and trying not to look longingly at the poultry; for he had set his heart on at least a skinny bird as a surprise to Kit.

Sammy's adventures that day had been more varied and his efforts more successful, as we shall see, in the end, for Sammy was a most engaging little fellow, and no one could look into his blue eyes without wanting to pat his curly yellow head with one hand while the other gave him something. The cares of life had not lessened his confidence in people; and only the most abandoned ruffians had the heart to deceive or disappoint him. His very tribulations usually led to something pleasant, and whatever happened, sunshiny Sam came right side up, lucky and laughing.

Undaunted by the drifts or the cold wind, he marched off with the remains of the old shovel to seek his fortune, and found it at the third house where he called. The first two sidewalks were easy jobs; and he pocketed his ninepences with a growing conviction that this was his chosen work. The third sidewalk was a fine long one, for the house stood on the corner, and two pavements must be cleared.

"It ought to be fifty cents; but perhaps they won't give me so much, I'm such a young one. I'll show 'em I can work, though, like a man;" and Sammy rang the bell with the energy of a telegraph boy.

Before the bell could be answered, a big boy rushed up, exclaiming roughly, "Get out of this! I'm going to have the job. You can't do it. Start, now, or I'll chuck you into a snow-bank."

"I won't!" answered Sammy, indignant at the brutal tone and unjust claim. "I got here first, and it's my job. You let me alone. I ain't afraid of you or your snow-banks either."

The big boy wasted no time in words, for steps were heard inside, but after a brief scuffle hauled Sammy, fighting bravely all the way, down the steps, and tumbled him into a deep drift. Then he ran up the steps, and respectfully asked for the job when a neat maid opened the door. He would have got it if Sam had not roared out, as he floundered in the drift, "I came first. He knocked me down 'cause I 'm the smallest. Please let me do it; please!"

Before another word could be said, a little old lady appeared in the hall, trying to look stern, and failing entirely, because she was the picture of a dear fat, cosey grandma.

"Send that *bad* big boy away, Maria, and call in the poor little fellow. I saw the whole thing, and *he* shall have the job if he can do it."

The bully slunk away, and Sammy came panting up the steps, white with snow, a great bruise on his forehead, and a beaming smile on his face, looking so like a jolly little Santa Claus who had taken a "header" out of his sleigh that the maid laughed, and the old lady exclaimed, "Bless the boy! he's dreadfully hurt, and doesn't know it. Come in and be brushed and get your breath, child, and tell me how that scamp came to treat you so."

Nothing loath to be comforted, Sammy told his little tale while Maria dusted him off on the mat, and the old lady hovered in the doorway of the dining-room, where a nice breakfast smoked and smelled so deliciously that the boy sniffed the odor of coffee and buckwheats like a hungry hound.

"He 'll get his death if he goes to work till he's dried a bit. Put him over the register, Maria, and I 'll give him a hot drink, for it's bitter cold, poor dear!"

Away trotted the kind old lady, and in a minute came back with coffee and cakes, on which Sammy feasted as he warmed his toes and told Kitty's plans for Christmas, led on by the old lady's questions, and quite unconscious that he was letting all sorts of cats out of the bag.

Mrs. Bryant understood the little story, and made her plans also, for the rosy-faced boy was very like a little grandson who died last year, and her sad old heart was very tender to all other small boys. So she found out where Sammy lived, and nodded and smiled at him most cheerily as he tugged stoutly away at the snow on the long pavements till all was done, and the little workman came for his wages.

A bright silver dollar and a pocketful of gingerbread sent him off a rich and happy boy to shovel and sweep till noon, when he proudly showed his earnings at home, and feasted the babies on the carefully hoarded cake, for Dilly and Dot were the idols of the household.

"Now, Sammy dear, I want you to take my place here this afternoon, for mother will have to take her work home by-and-by, and I must sell my wreaths. I only got enough green for six, and two bunches of holly; but if I can sell them for ten or twelve cents apiece, I shall be glad. Girls never *can* earn as much money as boys somehow," sighed Kitty, surveying the thin wreaths tied up with carpet ravellings, and vainly puzzling her young wits over a sad problem.

"I 'll give you some of my money if you don't get a dollar; then we'll be even. Men always take care of women, you know, and ought to," cried Sammy, setting a fine example to his father, if he had only been there to profit by it.

With thanks Kitty left him to rest on the old sofa, while the happy babies swarmed over him; and putting on the shabby hood and shawl, she slipped away to stand at the Park gate, modestly offering her little wares to the passers-by. A nice old gentleman bought two, and his wife scolded him for getting such bad ones; but the money gave more happiness than any other he spent that day. A child took a ten-cent bunch of holly with its red berries, and there Kitty's market ended. It was very cold, people were in a hurry, bolder hucksters pressed before the timid little girl, and the balloon man told her to "clear out."

Hoping for better luck, she tried several other places; but the short afternoon was soon over, the streets began to thin, the keen wind chilled her to the bone, and her heart was very heavy to think that in all the rich, merry city, where Christmas gifts passed her in every hand, there were none for the dear babies and boys at home, and the Christmas dinner was a failure.

"I must go and get supper anyway; and I 'll hang these up in our own rooms, as I can't sell them," said Kitty, wiping a very big tear from her cold cheek, and turning to go away.

A smaller, shabbier girl than herself stood near, looking at the bunch of holly with wistful eyes; and glad to do to others as she wished some one would do to her, Kitty offered the only thing she had to give, saying kindly, "You may have it; merry Christmas!" and ran away before the delighted child could thank her.

I am very sure that one of the spirits who fly about at this season of the year saw the little act, made a note of it, and in about fifteen minutes rewarded Kitty for her sweet remembrance of the golden rule.

As she went sadly homeward she looked up at some of the big houses where every window shone with the festivities of Christmas Eve, and more than one tear fell, for the little girl found life pretty hard just then.

"There don't seem to be any wreaths at these windows; perhaps they 'd buy mine. I can't bear to go home with so little for my share," she said, stopping before one of the biggest and brightest of these fairy palaces, where the sound of music was heard, and many little heads peeped from behind the curtains as if watching for some one.

Kitty was just going up the steps to make another trial, when two small boys came racing round the corner, slipped on the icy pavement, and both went down with a crash that would have broken older bones. One was up in a minute, laughing; the other lay squirming and howling, "Oh, my knee! my knee!" till Kitty ran and picked him up with the motherly consolations she had learned to give.

"It's broken; I know it is," wailed the small sufferer as Kitty carried him up the steps, while his friend wildly rang the doorbell.

It was like going into fairy-land, for the house was all astir with a children's Christmas party. Servants flew about with smiling faces; open doors gave ravishing glimpses of a feast in one room and a splendid tree in another; while a crowd of little faces peered over the balusters in the hall above, eager to come down and enjoy the glories prepared for them.

A pretty young girl came to meet Kitty, and listened to her story of the accident, which proved to be less severe than it at first appeared; for Bertie, the injured party, forgot his anguish at sight of the tree, and hopped upstairs so nimbly that every one laughed.

"He said his leg was broken, but I guess he's all right," said Kitty, reluctantly turning from this happy scene to go out into the night again.

"Would you like to see our tree before the children come down?" asked the pretty girl, seeing the wistful look in the child's eyes, and the shine of half-dried tears on her cheek.

"Oh, yes; I never saw anything so lovely. I'd like to tell the babies all about it;" and Kitty's face beamed at the prospect, as if the kind words had melted all the frost away.

"How many babies are there?" asked the pretty girl, as she led the way into the brilliant room. Kitty told her, adding several other facts, for the friendly atmosphere seemed to make them friends at once.

"I will buy the wreaths, for we haven't any," said the girl in silk, as Kitty told how she was just coming to offer them when the boys fell.

It was pretty to see how carefully the little hostess laid away the shabby garlands and slipped a half-dollar into Kitty's hand; prettier still, to watch the sly way in which she tucked some bonbons, a red ball, a blue whip, two china dolls, two pairs of little mittens, and some gilded nuts into an empty box for "the babies;" and prettiest of all, to see the smiles and tears make April in Kitty's face as she tried to tell her thanks for this beautiful surprise.

The world was all right when she got into the street again and ran home with the precious box hugged close, feeling that at last she had something to make a merry Christmas of.

Shrieks of joy greeted her, for Sammy's nice old lady had sent a basket full of pies, nuts and raisins, oranges and cake, and--oh, happy Sammy!--a sled, all for love of the blue eyes that twinkled so merrily when he told her about the tea-tray. Piled upon this red car of triumph, Dilly and Dot were being dragged about, while the other treasures were set forth on the table.

"I must show mine," cried Kitty; "we 'll look at them to-night, and have them to-morrow;" and amid more cries of rapture *her* box was unpacked, *her* money added to the pile in the middle of the table, where Sammy had laid his handsome contribution toward the turkey.

Before the story of the splendid tree was over, in came Tommy with his substantial offering and his hard-earned dollar.

"I 'm afraid I ought to keep my money for shoes. I 've walked the soles off these to-day, and can't go to school barefooted," he said, bravely trying to put the temptation of skates behind him.

"We 've got a good dinner without a turkey, and perhaps we 'd better not get it," added Kitty, with a sigh, as she surveyed the table, and remembered the blue knit hood marked seventy-five cents that she saw in a shop-window.

"Oh, we *must* have a turkey! we worked so hard for it, and it's so Christmasy," cried Sam, who always felt that pleasant things ought to happen.

"Must have turty," echoed the babies, as they eyed the dolls tenderly.

"You *shall* have a turkey, and there he is," said an unexpected voice, as a noble bird fell upon the table, and lay there kicking up his legs as if enjoying the surprise immensely.

It was father's voice, and there stood father, neither cross nor stupid, but looking as he used to look, kind and happy, and beside him was mother, smiling as they had not seen her smile for months. It was not because the work was well paid for, and more promised, but because she had received a gift that made the world bright, a home happy again,--father's promise to drink no more.

"I 've been working to-day as well as you, and you may keep your money for yourselves. There are shoes for all; and never again, please God, shall my children be ashamed of me, or want a dinner Christmas Day."

As father said this with a choke in his voice, and mother's head went down on his shoulder to hide the happy tears that wet her cheeks, the children didn't know whether to laugh or cry, till Kitty, with the instinct of a loving heart, settled the question by saying, as she held out her hands, "We haven't any tree, so let's dance around our goodies and be merry."

Then the tired feet in the old shoes forgot their weariness, and five happy little souls skipped gayly round the table, where, in the midst of all the treasures earned and given, father's Christmas turkey proudly lay in state.

Printed in Great Britain
by Amazon

13579865R00062